A STING IN THE TALE

An Anthology of Twist Endings

CONTENTS

INTRODUCTION

By M. M. Owen

The twist ending – an unanticipated conclusion which forces the audience to radically re-evaluate a piece's narrative, characterisation, or both – is a widely used and widely appreciated trope. Indeed, such climaxes have been delighting readers since before the Victorian Era, and nowadays occupy a unique space as something of a pseudo sub-genre.

In spite of this, few collections of those tales which have best utilised the narrative device have ever emerged. For this reason, this collection brings together nine of the greatest twist-bestowed tales, from the pens of seven different authors, with conclusions ingenious enough that even the most perceptive readers should not be able to prognosticate them.

*

The narrative twist has a long and noble history. Peripeteia – a dramatic technique in which the protagonist's fortunes are suddenly and sharply reversed – dates all the way back to Ancient Greece, where, upon seeing it displayed in Sophocles' Athenian tragedy *Oedipus Rex,* Aristotle declared it "The finest form of Discovery." In the New Testament, meanwhile, Paul the Apostle's instantaneous conversion to Christianity is a biblical twist which has since given the English language the well-known idiom "on the road to Damascus."

One of the oldest examples of a narrative twist deployed as an ending is in 'The Three Apples', a story taken from the collection of Islamic folk tales *One Thousand and One Nights.* First published in English in 1706, 'The Three Apples' sees its protagonist, Ja'far ibn Yahya embark on a mission which is archetypal of the modern 'whodunit' mystery. At the very climax of the narrative, Yahya discovers the truth behind the tale's mystery through sheer fluke, moments before he is scheduled for execution, thus saving his life.

Nowadays, the twist ending is a much more commonplace phenomenon. Cinema in particular – especially Alfred Hitchcock's masterworks *Vertigo* (1958) and *Psycho* (1960), Rod Serling's *The Twilight Zone,* (1959-1964) and, more recently, the successes of *The Crying Game* (1992) and *The Usual Suspects (1995)* – has developed something of a love affair with the shock ending. Indeed, the revealing of a twist to someone who hasn't already witnessed it (also known as a 'spoiler') is seen as a major breach of film-watching etiquette. Witness Dr. Cox in well-known American sitcom *Scrubs* taking revenge on the Janitor by telling him, midway through *The Sixth Sense* (1996), "Bruce Willis is a ghost; he's been dead the entire time."

Predictably, the increased popularity of twist endings – particularly on the screen, and particularly on the part of director M. Night Shyamalan – has reaped mixed results. So well-known are they now that it is just as easy for the narrative device to come off as asinine or cliché as it is for it to thrill or surprise. For all cinema's twist successes – *Mulholland Drive* (2001), *The Others* (2001), *Saw* (2004) – there have been a number of less-than-satisfactory examples: *Secret Window* (2004), *The Village* (2004) and *The Number 23* (2007), to name a few.

Similarly, on the page, twist endings have proliferated with mixed results in recent decades. Novels such as Iain Banks' *The Wasp Factory* (1984), Chuck Palahniuk's *Fight Club* (1996) and Ian McEwan's *Atonement* (2001) are vastly outnumbered by works which use the device in a somewhat contrived fashion. For commercial thriller writers such as Harlan Coben, the climatic twist is almost obligatory.

The stories in this collection, then, are from what might be considered 'the golden age' of the twist ending; a time when some of the finest authors of the day dedicated themselves, tale after tale, to perfecting their use of the narrative device. Spanning 70 years, the stories come out of a range of literary traditions, from Poe's Gothic to O. Henry's light-hearted social realism, but all of them share, as their climax, what two and a half millennia ago Aristotle dubbed "The finest form of Discovery."

The first author in this collection, Edgar Allen Poe, was a great fan of the twist ending. In fact, a number of his other tales - 'The Murders in the Rue Morgue' and 'The Cask of Amontillado', for example – could have been included here. As Poe laid out in his essay 'The Philosophy of Composition' (1846), he placed great importance on how a piece of work culminated. Little surprise, therefore, that he enjoyed utilising that most dramatic of endings: the twist.

'The Masque of the Red Death' (1842) includes a number of classic Gothic tropes, not least the castle setting and the air of imminent doom. Playing heavily on thanatophobic concerns, it is a heavily allegorical tale, with the various rooms of the palace standing in for the various stages of life and the ever-ringing clock symbolizing death's omnipresence. The twist brings The Red Death into focus as a sort of extreme egalitarianism, by which all men, whether extremely wealthy or dirt poor, are equal before the perils of disease.

'The Black Cat' (1843) reads like a condensed and more surreal *Crime and Punishment* (1866). Its protagonist is a frenetic and nervous man, who tells us that he "neither expect[s] nor solicit[s] belief" before going on to insist that he isn't mad. From there, the tale is essentially a study of the psychology of guilt, and the weighty, tortuous pressure it can place on a psyche. The climactic twist is interesting, and typical of Poe, by virtue of being at once rationally possible and hugely unlikely. The story also contains, interestingly, Poe's strongest denouncement of alcohol. As a young man, the author had been involved with the temperance movement, yet fell into alcoholism in later life. Attitudes such as that expressed in 'The Black Cat' would suggest that he detested his habit, even as it consumed and even – as some of his biographers maintain – killed him.

Strictly speaking, the climax of Frank R. Stockton's 'The Lady, or the Tiger?' (1882) might better be termed an 'open ending' rather than a twist, as it abruptly denies the reader any sort of dénouement. However, its conclusion was so radical at the time of its publication, and it remains such a famous tale, that it is impossible to leave it out of a collection of twist endings. The twist itself is an interesting one, as it leaves a question mark over the character of the princess: Faced with her Catch-22, would she rather see her lover alive, even if with another woman, or if she can't have him, can no-one? Like Paul the Apostle's "on the road to Damascus," "The Lady, or the Tiger?" now holds a place in the English language as shorthand for an unresolvable problem.

Guy de Maupassant's 'The Necklace' (1884) is a comparatively famous story with a comparatively famous climax. The twist itself is laced with irony, and implicitly extols both the virtue of honesty and the the danger of vanity – the entire situation develops because of Madame Mathilde Loisel's bourgeois aspirations, and the decade-long tragedy of the piece could have been avoided had she admitted her mistake. The story was the inspiration for Henry James' 'Paste', which cleverly inverts de Maupassant's version, and was dramatised professionally for the first time at the Edinburgh Festival in 2007.

Ambrose Bierce's 'An Occurrence at Owl Creek Bridge' (1890) possesses yet another well-known twist ending. Once called the "greatest American short story" and "a flawless example of American genius" by author Kurt Vonnegut, the story is loosely based on Bierce's own wartime experience – he spent almost all of the American Civil War (1861-1865) in infantry regiments of the Northern army, and fought in a number of major conflicts, including the Battle of Shiloh. Along with other works of its time, such as Stephen Crane's *The Red Badge of Courage* (1895), Bierce's story brought a new realism to the depiction of war in fiction. Read now, 'An Occurrence at Owl Creek Bridge' remains a surprisingly modern story, with its irregular time sequence, morally grey central event and blurring of conscious realities. Its climatic twist is notable for being not just surprising, but unexpectedly poignant, and the tale as a whole contains a wry nod to the adventure fiction of Bierce's day, which frequently featured seemingly impossible means of escape.

'The Case of Lady Sannox' (1893) was published at a time when Arthur Conan Doyle's Sherlock Holmes tales had recently made him a popular author with the reading public. For this reason, the story received a prominent place on the front cover of *The Idler*, the serial magazine in which it was first published. However, the tale itself doesn't feature the famous detective – Conan Doyle was already becoming tired of Holmes, and would kill him off just a month later in 'The Final Problem' (1893) – and is arguably the most horror-tinged of all the author's short works. The grisly twist ending plays into turn-of-the-century debates surrounding women and their legal status in society, and exhibits the cruelties made possible in a strict patriarchy.

Unlike most of his output, which was light-hearted in tone, W. W. Jacobs' 'The Monkey's Paw' (1902) is a macabre and unsettling tale. Essentially a grim take on the 'law of unintended consequences', it is now a classic of the horror genre which has been adapted numerous times across various mediums. As well as a classic short story, it is very much a parable in the Victorian moralistic mode, warning readers against (literally) tempting fate, and encouraging them to accept their lot. The familiar 'three wishes' format draws heavily on the tale of Aladdin and the magic lamp, taken from the *One Thousand and One Nights* referenced by Mrs. White (as "*Arabian* Nights") in the story.

The final two stories in this collection come from a fitting source. O. Henry – a pseudonym adopted by William Sydney Porter while in prison on charges of embezzlement – is arguably the most famous practitioner of the twist ending in all of literature. Indeed, many readers actually refer to the device as an 'O. Henry ending'. In his day, he was hailed as the American answer to Guy de Maupassant (author of 'The Necklace') precisely for the reason that he was viewed as capable of producing comparatively clever conclusions. In just a few short years of professional writing, Henry produced nearly three-hundred (usually twist-bestowed) short stories, and, for want of space, many others - 'The Cop and the Anthem' (1904) 'The Last Leaf' (1907), and 'A Retrieved Reformation' (1909), to name just three – could have appeared here.

Most of O. Henry's twists play on coincidental and lightly humorous circumstances, and contain twists which lead quickly into a brief dénouement. This is exemplified in 'The Gift of the Magi' (1906), an ironic and sentimental tale which has been adapted in various ways into more than ten separate films. Similarly, in 'The Ransom of Red Chief' (1910), the eventual climax of the plot inverts the reader's initial expectations in a way that has proved humorous enough for both Disney's *TaleSpin* series and *Denice the Menace* to adapt.

Together., these two tales form a fitting end to

the collection, providing a stark contrast in tone with the grisly twists of Conan Doyle and Jacobs' tales. They also represent a high-water mark in the craft of literary twist-composition; since O. Henry, arguably not a single other author – and certainly not over the short form – has dedicated themselves so consistently and carefully to producing such clever, unexpected conclusions.

*

Ultimately, the twist ending is a somewhat mercurial thing. Like many other well-known plot devices – the flashforward, the the breaking of the fourth wall – when deployed well, it can work to great effect. However, and nowadays more than ever, it can just as easily come off as fatuous and even detrimental if used badly.

The stories in this collection represent the very best examples of the device being put to use. If readers fail to predict the conclusions as they loom at the far end of the narrative, and if those conclusions succeed in eliciting surprise and reflection, then the authors have succeeded. If readers, in turn, enjoy the effect created by these twists, then they are encouraged to track down the many other (cinematic and literary) examples listed earlier. This collection, after all, is but an introduction to a narrative device with a long and colourful history, and a future in which the bar is set very, very high.

THE MASQUE OF RED DEATH

by Edgar Allan Poe

The "Red Death" had long devastated the country. No pestilence had ever been so fatal, or so hideous. Blood was its Avatar and its seal—the redness and the horror of blood. There were sharp pains, and sudden dizziness, and then profuse bleeding at the pores, with dissolution. The scarlet stains upon the body and especially upon the face of the victim, were the pest ban which shut him out from the aid and from the sympathy of his fellow-men. And the whole seizure, progress and termination of the disease, were the incidents of half an hour.

But the Prince Prospero was happy and dauntless and sagacious. When his dominions were half depopulated, he summoned to his presence a thousand hale and light-hearted friends from among the knights and dames of his court, and with these retired to the deep seclusion of one of his castellated abbeys. This was an extensive and magnificent structure, the creation of the prince's own eccentric yet august taste. A strong and lofty wall girdled it in. This wall had gates of iron. The courtiers, having entered, brought furnaces and massy hammers and welded the bolts. They resolved to leave means neither of ingress nor egress to the sudden impulses of despair or of frenzy from within. The abbey was amply provisioned. With such precautions the courtiers might bid defiance to contagion. The external world could take care of itself. In the meantime it was folly to grieve, or to think. The prince had provided all the appliances of pleasure. There were buffoons, there were improvisatori, there were ballet-dancers, there were musicians, there was Beauty, there was wine. All these and security were within. Without was the "Red Death".

It was towards the close of the fifth or sixth month of his seclusion, and while the pestilence raged most furiously abroad, that the Prince Prospero entertained his thousand friends at a masked ball of the most unusual magnificence.

It was a voluptuous scene, that masquerade. But first let me tell of the rooms in which it was held. These were seven—an imperial suite. In many palaces, however, such suites form a long and straight vista, while the folding doors slide back nearly to the walls on either hand, so that the view of the whole extent is scarcely impeded. Here the case was very different, as might have been expected from the duke's love of the bizarre. The apartments were so irregularly disposed that the vision embraced but little more than one at a time. There was a sharp turn at every twenty or thirty yards, and at each turn a novel effect. To the right and left, in the middle of each wall, a tall and narrow Gothic window looked out upon a closed corridor which pursued the windings of the suite. These windows were of stained glass whose colour varied in accordance with the prevailing hue of the decorations of the chamber into which it opened. That at the eastern extremity was hung, for example in blue—and vividly blue were its windows. The second chamber was purple in its ornaments and tapestries, and here the panes were purple. The third was green throughout, and so were the casements. The fourth was furnished and lighted with orange—the fifth with white—the sixth with violet. The seventh apartment was closely shrouded in black velvet tapestries that hung all over the ceiling and down the walls, falling in heavy folds upon a carpet of the same material and hue. But in this chamber only, the colour of the windows failed to correspond with the decorations. The panes here were scarlet—a deep blood colour. Now in no one of the seven apartments was there any lamp or candelabrum, amid the profusion of golden ornaments that lay scattered to and fro or depended from the roof. There was no light of any kind emanating from lamp or candle within the suite of chambers. But in the corridors that followed the suite, there stood, opposite to each window, a heavy tripod, bearing a brazier of fire, that projected its rays through the tinted glass and so glaringly illumined the room.

And thus were produced a multitude of gaudy and fantastic appearances. But in the western or black chamber the effect of the fire-light that streamed upon the dark hangings through the blood-tinted panes, was ghastly in the extreme, and produced so wild a look upon the countenances of those who entered, that there were few of the company bold enough to set foot within its precincts at all.

It was in this apartment, also, that there stood against the western wall, a gigantic clock of ebony. Its pendulum swung to and fro with a dull, heavy, monotonous clang; and when the minute-hand made the circuit of the face, and the hour was to be stricken, there came from the brazen lungs of the clock a sound which was clear and loud and deep and exceedingly musical, but of so peculiar a note and emphasis that, at each lapse of an hour, the musicians of the orchestra were constrained to pause, momentarily, in their performance, to harken to the sound; and thus the waltzers perforce ceased their evolutions; and there was a brief disconcert of the whole gay company; and, while the chimes of the clock yet rang, it was observed that the giddiest grew pale, and the more aged and sedate passed their hands over their brows as if in confused revery or meditation. But when the echoes had fully ceased, a light laughter at once pervaded the assembly; the musicians looked at each other and smiled as if at their own nervousness and folly, and made whispering vows, each to the other, that the next chiming of the clock should produce in them no similar emotion; and then, after the lapse of sixty minutes, (which embrace three thousand and six hundred seconds of the Time that flies,) there came yet another chiming of the clock, and then were the same disconcert and tremulousness and meditation as before.

But, in spite of these things, it was a gay and magnificent revel. The tastes of the duke were peculiar. He had a fine eye for colours and effects. He disregarded the decora of mere fashion. His plans were bold and fiery, and his conceptions glowed with barbaric lustre. There are some who would have thought him mad. His followers felt that he was not. It was necessary to hear and see and touch him to be sure that he was not.

He had directed, in great part, the movable embellishments of the seven chambers, upon occasion of this great fête; and it was his own guiding taste which had given character to the masqueraders. Be sure they were grotesque. There were much glare and glitter and piquancy and phantasm—much of what has been since seen in "Hernani". There were arabesque figures with unsuited limbs and appointments. There were delirious fancies such as the madman fashions. There were much of the beautiful, much of the wanton, much of the bizarre, something of the terrible, and not a little of that which might have excited disgust. To and fro in the seven chambers there stalked, in fact, a multitude of dreams. And these—the dreams—writhed in and about taking hue from the rooms, and causing the wild music of the orchestra to seem as the echo of their steps. And, anon, there strikes the ebony clock which stands in the hall of the velvet. And then, for a moment, all is still, and all is silent save the voice of the clock. The dreams are stiff-frozen as they stand. But the echoes of the chime die away—they have endured but an instant—and a light, half-subdued laughter floats after them as they depart. And now again the music swells, and the dreams live, and writhe to and fro more merrily than ever, taking hue from the many tinted windows through which stream the rays from the tripods. But to the chamber which lies most westwardly of the seven, there are now none of the maskers who venture; for the night is waning away; and there flows a ruddier light through the blood-coloured panes; and the blackness of the sable drapery appals; and to him whose foot falls upon the sable carpet, there comes from the near clock of ebony a muffled peal more solemnly emphatic than any which reaches their ears who indulged in the more remote gaieties of the other apartments.

But these other apartments were densely crowded, and in them beat feverishly the heart of life.

And the revel went whirlingly on, until at length there commenced the sounding of midnight upon the clock. And then the music ceased, as I have told; and the evolutions of the waltzers were quieted; and there was an uneasy cessation of all things as before. But now there were twelve strokes to be sounded by the bell of the clock; and thus it happened, perhaps, that more of thought crept, with more of time, into the meditations of the thoughtful among those who revelled. And thus too, it happened, perhaps, that before the last echoes of the last chime had utterly sunk into silence, there were many individuals in the crowd who had found leisure to become aware of the presence of a masked figure which had arrested the attention of no single individual before. And the rumour of this new presence having spread itself whisperingly around, there arose at length from the whole company a buzz, or murmur, expressive of disapprobation and surprise—then, finally, of terror, of horror, and of disgust.

In an assembly of phantasms such as I have

painted, it may well be supposed that no ordinary appearance could have excited such sensation. In truth the masquerade licence of the night was nearly unlimited; but the figure in question had out-Heroded Herod, and gone beyond the bounds of even the prince's indefinite decorum. There are chords in the hearts of the most reckless which cannot be touched without emotion. Even with the utterly lost, to whom life and death are equally jests, there are matters of which no jest can be made. The whole company, indeed, seemed now deeply to feel that in the costume and bearing of the stranger neither wit nor propriety existed. The figure was tall and gaunt, and shrouded from head to foot in the habiliments of the grave. The mask which concealed the visage was made so nearly to resemble the countenance of a stiffened corpse that the closest scrutiny must have had difficulty in detecting the cheat. And yet all this might have been endured, if not approved, by the mad revellers around. But the mummer had gone so far as to assume the type of the Red Death. His vesture was dabbled in blood—and his broad brow, with all the features of the face, was besprinkled with the scarlet horror.

When the eyes of the Prince Prospero fell upon this spectral image (which, with a slow and solemn movement, as if more fully to sustain its role, stalked to and fro among the waltzers) he was seen to be convulsed, in the first moment with a strong shudder either of terror or distaste; but, in the next, his brow reddened with rage.

"Who dares,"—he demanded hoarsely of the courtiers who stood near him—"who dares insult us with this blasphemous mockery? Seize him and unmask him—that we may know whom we have to hang, at sunrise, from the battlements!"

It was in the eastern or blue chamber in which stood the Prince Prospero as he uttered these words. They rang throughout the seven rooms loudly and clearly, for the prince was a bold and robust man, and the music had become hushed at the waving of his hand.

It was in the blue room where stood the

prince, with a group of pale courtiers by his side. At first, as he spoke, there was a slight rushing movement of this group in the direction of the intruder, who at the moment was also near at hand, and now, with deliberate and stately step, made closer approach to the speaker. But from a certain nameless awe with which the mad assumptions of the mummer had inspired the whole party, there were found none who put forth hand to seize him; so that, unimpeded, he passed within a yard of the prince's person; and, while the vast assembly, as if with one impulse, shrank from the centres of the rooms to the walls, he made his way uninterruptedly, but with the same solemn and measured step which had distinguished him from the first, through the blue chamber to the purple—through the purple to the green—through the green to the orange—through this again to the white—and even thence to the violet, ere a decided movement had been made to arrest him. It was then, however, that the Prince Prospero, maddening with rage and the shame of his own momentary cowardice, rushed hurriedly through the six chambers, while none followed him on account of a deadly terror that had seized upon all. He bore aloft a drawn dagger, and had approached, in rapid impetuosity, to within three or four feet of the retreating figure, when the latter, having attained the extremity of the velvet apartment, turned suddenly and confronted his pursuer. There was a sharp cry—and the dagger dropped gleaming upon the sable carpet, upon which, instantly afterwards, fell prostrate in death the Prince Prospero. Then, summoning the wild courage of despair, a throng of the revellers at once threw themselves into the black apartment, and, seizing the mummer, whose tall figure stood erect and motionless within the shadow of the ebony clock, gasped in unutterable horror at finding the grave cerements and corpse-like mask, which they handled with so violent a rudeness, untenanted by any tangible form.

And now was acknowledged the presence of the Red Death. He had come like a thief in the night. And one by one dropped the revellers in the blood-bedewed halls of their revel, and died each in the despairing posture of his fall. And the life of the ebony clock went out with that of the last of the gay. And the flames of the tripods expired. And Darkness and Decay and the Red Death held illimitable dominion over all.

THE BLACK CAT

by Edgar Allen Poe

For the most wild, yet most homely narrative which I am about to pen, I neither expect nor solicit belief. Mad indeed would I be to expect it, in a case where my very senses reject their own evidence. Yet, mad am I not—and very surely do I not dream. But to-morrow I die, and to-day I would unburthen my soul. My immediate purpose is to place before the world, plainly, succinctly, and without comment, a series of mere household events. In their consequences, these events have terrified—have tortured—have destroyed me. Yet I will not attempt to expound them. To me, they have presented little but Horror—to many they will seem less terrible than barroques. Hereafter, perhaps, some intellect may be found which will reduce my phantasm to the common-place—some intellect more calm, more logical, and far less excitable than my own, which will perceive, in the circumstances I detail with awe, nothing more than an ordinary succession of very natural causes and effects.

From my infancy I was noted for the docility and humanity of my disposition. My tenderness of heart was even so conspicuous as to make me the jest of my companions. I was especially fond of animals, and was indulged by my parents with a great variety of pets. With these I spent most of my time, and never was so happy as when feeding and caressing them. This peculiarity of character grew with my growth, and in my manhood, I derived from it one of my principal sources of pleasure. To those who have cherished an affection for a faithful and sagacious dog, I need hardly be at the trouble of explaining the nature or the intensity of the gratification thus derivable. There is something in the unselfish and self-sacrificing love of a brute, which goes directly to the heart of him who has had frequent occasion to test the paltry friendship and gossamer fidelity of mere Man.

I married early, and was happy to find in my

wife a disposition not uncongenial with my own. Observing my partiality for domestic pets, she lost no opportunity of procuring those of the most agreeable kind. We had birds, gold-fish, a fine dog, rabbits, a small monkey, and a cat.

This latter was a remarkably large and beautiful animal, entirely black, and sagacious to an astonishing degree. In speaking of his intelligence, my wife, who at heart was not a little tinctured with superstition, made frequent allusion to the ancient popular notion, which regarded all black cats as witches in disguise. Not that she was ever serious upon this point—and I mention the matter at all for no better reason than that it happens, just now, to be remembered.

Pluto—this was the cat's name—was my favorite pet and playmate. I alone fed him, and he attended me wherever I went about the house. It was even with difficulty that I could prevent him from following me through the streets.

Our friendship lasted, in this manner, for

several years, during which my general temperament and character—through the instrumentality of the Fiend Intemperance—had (I blush to confess it) experienced a radical alteration for the worse. I grew, day by day, more moody, more irritable, more regardless of the feelings of others. I suffered myself to use intemperate language to my wife. At length, I even offered her personal violence. My pets, of course, were made to feel the change in my disposition. I not only neglected, but ill-used them. For Pluto, however, I still retained sufficient regard to restrain me from maltreating him, as I made no scruple of maltreating the rabbits, the monkey, or even the dog, when by accident, or through affection, they came in my way. But my disease grew upon me—for what disease is like Alcohol!—and at length even Pluto, who was now becoming old, and consequently somewhat peevish—even Pluto began to experience the effects of my ill temper.

One night, returning home, much intoxicated, from one of my haunts about town, I fancied that the cat avoided my presence. I seized him; when, in his fright at my violence, he inflicted a slight wound upon my hand with his teeth. The fury of a demon instantly possessed me. I knew myself no longer. My original soul seemed, at once, to take its flight from my body and a more than fiendish malevolence, gin-nurtured, thrilled every fibre of my frame. I took from my waistcoat-pocket a pen-knife, opened it, grasped the poor beast by the throat, and deliberately cut one of its eyes from the socket! I blush, I burn, I shudder, while I pen the damnable atrocity.

When reason returned with the morning—when I had slept off the fumes of the night's debauch—I experienced a sentiment half of horror, half of remorse, for the crime of which I had been guilty; but it was, at best, a feeble and equivocal feeling, and the soul remained untouched. I again plunged into excess, and soon drowned in wine all memory of the deed.

In the meantime the cat slowly recovered. The socket of the lost eye presented, it is true, a frightful appearance, but he no longer appeared to suffer any pain. He went about the house as usual, but, as might be expected, fled in extreme terror at my approach. I had so much of my old heart left, as to be at first grieved by this evident dislike on the part of a creature which had once so loved me. But this feeling soon gave place to irritation. And then came, as if to my final and irrevocable overthrow, the spirit of perverseness. Of this spirit philosophy takes no account. Yet I am not more sure that my soul lives, than I am that perverseness is one of the primitive impulses of the human heart—one of the indivisible primary faculties, or sentiments, which give direction to the character of Man. Who has not, a hundred times, found himself committing a vile or a silly action, for no other reason than because he knows he should not? Have we not a perpetual inclination, in the teeth of our best judgment, to violate that which is Law, merely because we understand it to be such? This spirit of perverseness, I say, came to my final overthrow. It was this unfathomable longing of the soul to vex itself—to offer violence to its own nature—to do wrong for the wrong's sake only—that urged me to continue and finally to consummate the injury I had inflicted upon the unoffending brute. One morning, in cool blood, I slipped a noose about its neck and hung it to the limb of a tree;—hung it with the tears streaming from my eyes, and with the bitterest remorse at my heart;—hung it because I knew that it had loved me, and because I felt it had given me no reason of offence;—hung it because I knew that in so doing I was committing a sin—a deadly sin that would so jeopardize my immortal soul as to place it—if such a thing wore possible—even beyond the reach of the infinite mercy of the Most Merciful and Most Terrible God.

On the night of the day on which this cruel deed was done, I was aroused from sleep by the cry of fire. The curtains of my bed were in flames. The whole house was blazing. It was with great difficulty that my wife, a servant, and myself, made our escape from the conflagration. The destruction was complete. My entire worldly wealth was swallowed up, and I resigned myself thenceforward to despair.

I am above the weakness of seeking to establish a sequence of cause and effect, between the disaster and the atrocity. But I am detailing a chain of facts—and wish not to leave even a possible link imperfect. On the day succeeding the fire, I visited the ruins. The walls, with one exception, had fallen in. This exception was found in a compartment wall, not very thick, which stood about the middle of the house, and against which had rested the head of my bed. The plastering had here, in great measure, resisted the action of the fire—a fact which I attributed to its having been recently spread. About this wall a dense crowd were collected, and many persons seemed to be examining a particular portion of it with very minute and eager attention. The words "strange!" "singular!" and other similar expressions, excited my curiosity. I approached and saw, as if graven in bas relief upon the white surface, the figure of a gigantic cat. The impression was given with an accuracy truly marvellous. There was a rope about the animal's neck.

When I first beheld this apparition—for I could scarcely regard it as less—my wonder and my terror were extreme. But at length reflection came to my aid. The cat, I remembered, had been hung in a garden adjacent to the house. Upon the alarm of fire, this garden had been immediately filled by the crowd—by some one of whom the animal must have been cut from the tree and thrown, through an open window, into my chamber. This had probably been done with the view of arousing me from sleep. The falling of other walls had compressed the victim of my cruelty into the substance of the freshly-spread plaster; the lime of which, with the flames, and the ammonia from the carcass, had then accomplished the portraiture as I saw it.

Although I thus readily accounted to my reason, if not altogether to my conscience, for the startling fact just detailed, it did not the less fail to make a deep impression upon my fancy. For months I could not rid myself of the phantasm of the cat; and, during this period, there came back into my spirit a half-sentiment that seemed, but was not, remorse. I went so far as to regret the loss of the animal, and to look about me, among the vile haunts which I now habitually frequented, for another pet of the same species, and of somewhat similar appearance, with which to supply its place.

One night as I sat, half stupified, in a den of more than infamy, my attention was suddenly drawn to some black object, reposing upon the head of one of the immense hogsheads of Gin, or of Rum, which constituted the chief furniture of the apartment. I had been looking steadily at the top of this hogshead for some minutes, and what now caused me surprise was the fact that I had not sooner perceived the object thereupon. I approached it, and touched it with my hand. It was a black cat—a very large one—fully as large as Pluto, and closely resembling him in every respect but one. Pluto had not a white hair upon any portion of his body; but this cat had a large, although indefinite splotch of white, covering nearly the whole region of the breast. Upon my touching him, he immediately arose, purred loudly, rubbed against my hand, and appeared delighted with my notice. This, then, was the very creature of which I was in search. I at once offered to purchase it of the landlord; but this person made no claim to it—knew nothing of it—had never seen it before.

I continued my caresses, and, when I prepared to go home, the animal evinced a disposition to accompany me. I permitted it to do so; occasionally stooping and patting it as I proceeded. When it reached the house it domesticated itself at once, and became immediately a great favorite with my wife.

For my own part, I soon found a dislike to it arising within me. This was just the reverse of what I had anticipated; but—I know not how or why it was—its evident fondness for myself rather disgusted and annoyed. By slow degrees, these feelings of disgust and annoyance rose into the bitterness of hatred. I avoided the creature; a certain sense of shame, and the remembrance of my former deed of cruelty, preventing me from physically abusing it. I did not, for some weeks, strike, or otherwise violently ill use it; but gradually—very gradually—I came to look upon it with unutterable loathing, and to flee silently from its odious presence, as from the breath of a pestilence.

What added, no doubt, to my hatred of the beast, was the discovery, on the morning after I brought it home, that, like Pluto, it also had been deprived of one of its eyes. This circumstance, however, only endeared it to my wife, who, as I have already said, possessed, in a high degree, that humanity of feeling which had once been my distinguishing trait, and the source of many of my simplest and purest pleasures.

With my aversion to this cat, however, its partiality for myself seemed to increase. It followed my footsteps with a pertinacity which it would be difficult to make the reader comprehend. Whenever I sat, it would crouch beneath my chair, or spring upon my knees, covering me with its loathsome caresses. If I arose to walk it would get between my feet and thus nearly throw me down, or, fastening its long and sharp claws in my dress, clamber, in this manner, to my breast. At such times, although I longed to destroy it with a blow, I was yet withheld from so doing, partly by a memory of my former crime, but chiefly—let me confess it at once—by absolute dread of the beast.

This dread was not exactly a dread of physical evil—and yet I should be at a loss how otherwise to define it. I am almost ashamed to own—yes, even in this felon's cell, I am almost ashamed to own—that the terror and horror with which the animal inspired me, had been heightened by one of the merest chimaeras it would be possible to conceive. My wife had called my attention, more than once, to the character of the mark of white hair, of which I have spoken, and which constituted the sole visible difference between the strange beast and the one I had destroyed. The reader will remember that this mark, although large, had been originally very indefinite; but, by slow degrees—degrees nearly imperceptible, and which for a long time my Reason struggled to reject as fanciful—it had, at length, assumed a rigorous distinctness of outline. It was now the representation of an object that I shudder to name—and for this, above all, I loathed, and dreaded, and would have rid myself of the monster had I dared—it was now, I say, the image of a hideous—of a ghastly thing—of the gallows!—oh, mournful and terrible engine of Horror and of Crime—of Agony and of Death!

And now was I indeed wretched beyond the wretchedness of mere Humanity. And a brute beast — whose fellow I had contemptuously destroyed—a brute beast to work out for me—for me a man, fashioned in the image of the High God—so much of insufferable wo! Alas! neither by day nor by night knew I the blessing of Rest any more! During the former the creature left me no moment alone; and, in the latter, I started, hourly, from dreams of unutterable fear, to find the hot breath of the thing upon my face, and its vast weight—an incarnate Night-Mare that I had no power to shake off—incumbent eternally upon my heart!

Beneath the pressure of torments such as these, the feeble remnant of the good within me succumbed. Evil thoughts became my sole intimates—the darkest and most evil of thoughts. The moodiness of my usual temper increased to hatred of all things and of all mankind; while, from the sudden, frequent, and ungovernable outbursts of a fury to which I now blindly abandoned myself, my uncomplaining wife, alas! was the most usual and the most patient of sufferers.

One day she accompanied me, upon some household errand, into the cellar of the old building which our poverty compelled us to inhabit. The cat followed me down the steep stairs, and, nearly throwing me headlong, exasperated me to madness. Uplifting an axe, and forgetting, in my wrath, the childish dread which had hitherto stayed my hand, I aimed a blow at the animal which, of course, would have proved instantly fatal had it descended as I wished. But this blow was arrested by the hand of my wife. Goaded, by the interference, into a rage more than demoniacal, I withdrew my arm from her grasp and buried the axe in her brain. She fell dead upon the spot, without a groan.

This hideous murder accomplished, I set myself forthwith, and with entire deliberation, to the task of concealing the body. I knew that I could not remove it from the house, either by day or by night, without the risk of being observed by the neighbors. Many projects entered my mind. At one period I thought of cutting the corpse into minute fragments, and destroying them by fire. At another, I resolved to dig a grave for it in the floor of the cellar. Again, I deliberated about casting it in the well in the yard—about packing it in a box, as if merchandize, with the usual arrangements, and so getting a porter to take it from the house. Finally I hit upon what I considered a far better expedient than either of these. I determined to wall it up in the cellar—as the monks of the middle ages are recorded to have walled up their victims.

For a purpose such as this the cellar was well

adapted. Its walls were loosely constructed, and had lately been plastered throughout with a rough plaster, which the dampness of the atmosphere had prevented from hardening. Moreover, in one of the walls was a projection, caused by a false chimney, or fireplace, that had been filled up, and made to resemble the red of the cellar. I made no doubt that I could readily displace the bricks at this point, insert the corpse, and wall the whole up as before, so that no eye could detect any thing suspicious. And in this calculation I was not deceived. By means of a crow-bar I easily dislodged the bricks, and, having carefully deposited the body against the inner wall, I propped it in that position, while, with little trouble, I re-laid the whole structure as it originally stood. Having procured mortar, sand, and hair, with every possible precaution, I prepared a plaster which could not be distinguished from the old, and with this I very carefully went over the new brickwork. When I had finished, I felt satisfied that all was right. The wall did not present the slightest appearance of having been disturbed. The rubbish on the floor was picked up with the minutest care. I looked around triumphantly, and said to myself—"Here at least, then, my labor has not been in vain."

My next step was to look for the beast which had been the cause of so much wretchedness; for I had, at length, firmly resolved to put it to death. Had I been able to meet with it, at the moment, there could have been no doubt of its fate; but it appeared that the crafty animal had been alarmed at the violence of my previous anger, and forebore to present itself in my present mood. It is impossible to describe, or to imagine, the deep, the blissful sense of relief which the absence of the detested creature occasioned in my bosom. It did not make its appearance during the night—and thus for one night at least, since its introduction into the house, I soundly and tranquilly slept; aye, slept even with the burden of murder upon my soul!

The second and the third day passed, and still my tormentor came not. Once again I breathed as a freeman. The monster, in terror, had fled the premises forever! I should behold it no more! My happiness was supreme! The guilt of my dark deed disturbed me but little. Some few inquiries had been made, but these had been readily answered. Even a search had been instituted—but of course nothing was to be discovered. I looked upon my future felicity as secured.

Upon the fourth day of the assassination, a party of the police came, very unexpectedly, into the house, and proceeded again to make rigorous investigation of the premises. Secure, however, in the inscrutability of my place of concealment, I felt no embarrassment whatever. The officers bade me accompany them in their search. They left no nook or corner unexplored. At length, for the third or fourth time, they descended into the cellar. I quivered not in a muscle. My heart beat calmly as that of one who slumbers in innocence. I walked the cellar from end to end. I folded my arms upon my bosom, and roamed easily to and fro. The police were thoroughly satisfied and prepared to depart. The glee at my heart was too strong to be restrained. I burned to say if but one word, by way of triumph, and to render doubly sure their assurance of my guiltlessness.

"Gentlemen," I said at last, as the party ascended the steps, "I delight to have allayed your suspicions. I wish you all health, and a little more courtesy. By the bye, gentlemen, this—this is a very well constructed house." [In the rabid desire to say something easily, I scarcely knew what I uttered at all.]—"I may say an excellently well constructed house. These walls are you going, gentlemen?—these walls are solidly put together;" and here, through the mere frenzy of bravado, I rapped heavily, with a cane which I held in my hand, upon that very portion of the brick-work behind which stood the corpse of the wife of my bosom.

But may God shield and deliver me from the fangs of the Arch-Fiend! No sooner had the reverberation of my blows sunk into silence, than I was answered by a voice from within the tomb!—by a cry, at first muffled and broken, like the sobbing of a child, and then quickly swelling into one long, loud, and continuous scream, utterly anomalous and inhuman—a howl—a wailing shriek, half of horror and half of triumph, such as might have arisen only out of hell, conjointly from the throats of the dammed in their agony and of the demons that exult in the damnation.

Of my own thoughts it is folly to speak. Swooning, I staggered to the opposite wall. For one instant the party upon the stairs remained motionless, through extremity of terror and of awe. In the next, a dozen stout arms were toiling at the wall. It fell bodily. The corpse, already greatly decayed and clotted with gore, stood erect before the eyes of the spectators. Upon its head, with red extended mouth and solitary eye of fire, sat the hideous beast whose craft had seduced me into murder, and whose informing voice had consigned me to the hangman. I had walled the monster up within the tomb!

THE LADY, OR THE TIGER?

by Frank R. Stockton

In the very olden time there lived a semi-barbaric king, whose ideas, though somewhat polished and sharpened by the progressiveness of distant Latin neighbors, were still large, florid, and untrammeled, as became the half of him which was barbaric. He was a man of exuberant fancy, and, withal, of an authority so irresistible that, at his will, he turned his varied fancies into facts. He was greatly given to self-communing, and, when he and himself agreed upon anything, the thing was done. When every member of his domestic and political systems moved smoothly in its appointed course, his nature was bland and genial; but, whenever there was a little hitch, and some of his orbs got out of their orbits, he was blander and more genial still, for nothing pleased him so much as to make the crooked straight and crush down uneven places.

Among the borrowed notions by which his barbarism had become semified was that of the public arena, in which, by exhibitions of manly and beastly valor, the minds of his subjects were refined and cultured.

But even here the exuberant and barbaric fancy asserted itself The arena of the king was built, not to give the people an opportunity of hearing the rhapsodies of dying gladiators, nor to enable them to view the inevitable conclusion of a conflict between religious opinions and hungry jaws, but for purposes far better adapted to widen and develop the mental energies of the people. This vast amphitheater, with its encircling galleries, its mysterious vaults, and its unseen passages, was an agent of poetic justice, in which crime was punished, or virtue rewarded, by the decrees of an impartial and incorruptible chance.

When a subject was accused of a crime of sufficient importance to interest the king, public notice was given that on an appointed day the fate of the accused person would be decided in the king's arena, a structure which well deserved its name, for, although its form and plan were borrowed from afar, its purpose emanated solely from the brain of this man, who, every barleycorn a king, knew no tradition to which he owed more allegiance than pleased his fancy, and who ingrafted on every adopted form of human thought and action the rich growth of his barbaric idealism.

When all the people had assembled in the galleries, and the king, surrounded by his court, sat high up on his throne of royal state on one side of the arena, he gave a signal, a door beneath him opened, and the accused subject stepped out into the amphitheater. Directly opposite him, on the other side of the inclosed space, were two doors, exactly alike and side by side. It was the duty and the privilege of the person on trial to walk directly to these doors and open one of them. He could open either door he pleased; he was subject to no guidance or influence but that of the aforementioned impartial and incorruptible chance. If he opened the one, there came out of it a hungry tiger, the fiercest and most cruel that could be procured, which immediately sprang upon him and tore him to pieces as a punishment for his guilt. The moment that the case of the criminal was thus decided, doleful iron bells were clanged, great wails went up from the hired mourners posted on the outer rim of the arena, and the vast audience, with bowed heads and downcast hearts, wended slowly their homeward way, mourning greatly that one so young and fair, or so old and respected, should have merited so dire a fate.

But, if the accused person opened the other door, there came forth from it a lady, the most suitable to his years and station that his majesty could select among his fair subjects, and to this lady he was immediately married, as a reward of his innocence. It mattered not that he might already possess a wife and family, or that his affections might be engaged upon an object of his own selection; the king allowed no such subordinate arrangements to interfere with his great scheme of retribution and reward. The exercises, as in the other instance, took place immediately, and in the arena. Another door opened beneath the king, and a priest, followed by a band of choristers, and dancing maidens blowing joyous airs on golden horns and treading an epithalamic measure, advanced to where the pair stood, side by side, and the wedding was promptly and cheerily solemnized. Then the gay brass bells rang forth their merry peals, the people shouted glad hurrahs, and the innocent man, preceded by children strewing flowers on his path, led his bride to his home.

This was the king's semi-barbaric method of administering justice. Its perfect fairness is obvious. The criminal could not know out of which door would come the lady; he opened either he pleased, without having the slightest idea whether, in the next instant, he was to be devoured or married. On some occasions the tiger came out of one door, and on some out of the other. The decisions of this tribunal were not only fair, they were positively determinate: the accused person was instantly punished if he found himself guilty, and, if innocent, he was rewarded on the spot, whether he liked it or not. There was no escape from the judgments of the king's arena.

The institution was a very popular one. When the people gathered together on one of the great trial days, they never knew whether they were to witness a bloody slaughter or a hilarious wedding. This element of uncertainty lent an interest to the occasion which it could not otherwise have attained. Thus, the masses were entertained and pleased, and the thinking part of the community could bring no charge of unfairness against this plan, for did not the accused person have the whole matter in his own hands?

This semi-barbaric king had a daughter as blooming as his most florid fancies, and with a soul as fervent and imperious as his own. As is usual in such cases, she was the apple of his eye, and was loved by him above all humanity. Among his courtiers was a young man of that fineness of blood and lowness of station common to the conventional heroes of romance who love royal maidens. This royal maiden was well satisfied with her lover, for he was handsome and brave to a degree unsurpassed in all this kingdom, and she loved him with an ardor that had enough of barbarism in it to make it exceedingly warm and strong. This love affair moved on happily for many months, until one day the king happened to discover its existence. He did not hesitate nor waver in regard to his duty in the premises. The youth was immediately cast into prison, and a day was appointed for his trial in the king's arena. This, of course, was an especially important occasion, and his majesty, as well as all the people, was greatly interested in the workings and development of this trial. Never before had such a case occurred; never before had a subject dared to love the daughter of the king. In after years such things became commonplace enough, but then they were in no slight degree novel and startling.

The tiger-cages of the kingdom were searched for the most savage and relentless beasts, from which the fiercest monster might be selected for the arena; and the ranks of maiden youth and beauty throughout the land were carefully surveyed by competent judges in order that the young man might have a fitting bride in case fate did not determine for him a different destiny. Of course, everybody knew that the deed with which the accused was charged had been done. He had loved the princess, and neither he, she, nor any one else, thought of denying the fact; but the king would not think of allowing any fact of this kind to interfere with the workings of the tribunal, in which he took such great delight and satisfaction. No matter how the affair turned out, the youth would be disposed of, and the king would take anaesthetic pleasure in watching the course of events, which would determine whether or not the young man had done wrong in allowing himself to love the princess.

The appointed day arrived. From far and near the people gathered, and thronged the great galleries of the arena, and crowds, unable to gain admittance, massed themselves against its outside walls. The king and his court were in their places, opposite the twin doors, those fateful portals, so terrible in their similarity.

All was ready. The signal was given. A door beneath the royal party opened, and the lover of the princess walked into the arena. Tall, beautiful, fair, his appearance was greeted with a low hum of admiration and anxiety. Half the audience had not known so grand a youth had lived among them. No wonder the princess loved him! What a terrible thing for him to be there!

As the youth advanced into the arena he turned, as the custom was, to bow to the king, but he did not think at all of that royal personage. His eyes were fixed upon the princess, who sat to the right of her father. Had it not been for the moiety of barbarism in her nature it is probable that lady would not have been there, but her intense and fervid soul would not allow her to be absent on an occasion in which she was so terribly interested. From the moment that the decree had gone forth that her lover should decide his fate in the king's arena, she had thought of nothing, night or day, but this great event and the various subjects connected with it. Possessed of more power, influence, and force of character than any one who had ever before been interested in such a case, she had done what no other person had done—she had possessed herself of the secret of the doors. She knew in which of the two rooms, that lay behind those doors, stood the cage of the tiger, with its open front, and in which waited the lady. Through these thick doors, heavily curtained with skins on the inside, it was impossible that any noise or suggestion should come from within to the person who should approach to raise the latch of one of them. But gold, and the power of a woman's will, had brought the secret to the princess.

And not only did she know in which room stood the lady ready to emerge, all blushing and radiant, should her door be opened, but she knew who the lady was. It was one of the fairest and loveliest of the damsels of the court who had been selected as the reward of the accused youth, should he be proved innocent of the crime of aspiring to one so far above him; and the princess hated her. Often had she seen, or imagined that she had seen, this fair creature throwing glances of admiration upon the person of her lover, and sometimes she thought these glances were perceived, and even returned. Now and then she had seen them talking together; it was but for a moment or two, but much can be said in a brief space; it may have been on most unimportant topics, but how could she know that? The girl was lovely, but she had dared to raise her eyes to the loved one of the princess; and, with all the intensity of the savage blood transmitted to her through long lines of wholly barbaric ancestors, she hated the woman who blushed and trembled behind that silent door.

When her lover turned and looked at her, and his eye met hers as she sat there, paler and whiter than any one in the vast ocean of anxious faces about her, he saw, by that power of quick perception which is given to those whose souls are one, that she knew behind which door crouched the tiger, and behind which stood the lady. He had expected her to know it.

He understood her nature, and his soul was assured that she would never rest until she had made plain to herself this thing, hidden to all other lookers-on, even to the king. The only hope for the youth in which there was any element of certainty was based upon the success of the princess in discovering this mystery; and the moment he looked upon her, he saw she had succeeded, as in his soul he knew she would succeed.

Then it was that his quick and anxious glance asked the question: "Which?" It was as plain to her as if he shouted it from where he stood. There was not an instant to be lost. The question was asked in a flash; it must be answered in another.

Her right arm lay on the cushioned parapet before her. She raised her hand, and made a slight, quick movement toward the right. No one but her lover saw her. Every eye but his was fixed on the man in the arena.

He turned, and with a firm and rapid step he walked across the empty space. Every heart stopped beating, every breath was held, every eye was fixed immovably upon that man. Without the slightest hesitation, he went to the door on the right, and opened it.

Now, the point of the story is this: Did the tiger come out of that door, or did the lady ?

The more we reflect upon this question, the harder it is to answer. It involves a study of the human heart which leads us through devious mazes of passion, out of which it is difficult to find our way. Think of it, fair reader, not as if the decision of the question depended upon yourself, but upon that hot-blooded, semi-barbaric princess, her soul at a white heat beneath the combined fires of despair and jealousy. She had lost him, but who should have him?

How often, in her waking hours and in her dreams, had she started in wild horror, and covered her face with her hands as she thought of her lover opening the door on the other side of which waited the cruel fangs of the tiger!

But how much oftener had she seen him at the other door! How in her grievous reveries had she

gnashed her teeth, and torn her hair, when she saw his start of rapturous delight as he opened the door of the lady! How her soul had burned in agony when she had seen him rush to meet that woman, with her flushing cheek and sparkling eye of triumph; when she had seen him lead her forth, his whole frame kindled with the joy of recovered life; when she had heard the glad shouts from the multitude, and the wild
ringing of the happy bells; when she had seen the priest, with his joyous followers, advance to the couple, and make them man and wife before her very eyes; and when she had seen them walk away together upon their path of flowers, followed by the tremendous shouts of the hilarious multitude, in which her one despairing shriek was lost and drowned!

Would it not be better for him to die at once, and go to wait for her in the blessed regions of semi-barbaric futurity?

And yet, that awful tiger, those shrieks, that blood!

Her decision had been indicated in an instant,

but it had been made after days and nights of anguished deliberation. She had known she would be asked, she had decided what she would answer, and, without the slightest hesitation, she had moved her hand to the right.

The question of her decision is one not to be lightly considered, and it is not for me to presume to set myself up as the one person able to answer it. And so I leave it with all of you: Which came out of the opened door—the lady, or the tiger?

THE NECKLACE

by Guy de Maupassant

The girl was one of those pretty and charming young creatures who sometimes are born, as if by a slip of fate, into a family of clerks. She had no dowry, no expectations, no way of being known, understood, loved, married by any rich and distinguished man; so she let herself be married to a little clerk of the Ministry of Public Instruction.

She dressed plainly because she could not dress well, but she was unhappy as if she had really fallen from a higher station; since with women there is neither caste nor rank, for beauty, grace and charm take the place of family and birth. Natural ingenuity, instinct for what is elegant, a supple mind are their sole hierarchy, and often make of women of the people the equals of the very greatest ladies.

Mathilde suffered ceaselessly, feeling herself

born to enjoy all delicacies and all luxuries. She was distressed at the poverty of her dwelling, at the bareness of the walls, at the shabby chairs, the ugliness of the curtains. All those things, of which another woman of her rank would never even have been conscious, tortured her and made her angry. The sight of the little Breton peasant who did her humble housework aroused in her despairing regrets and bewildering dreams. She thought of silent antechambers hung with Oriental tapestry, illumined by tall bronze candelabra, and of two great footmen in knee breeches who sleep in the big armchairs, made drowsy by the oppressive heat of the stove. She thought of long reception halls hung with ancient silk, of the dainty cabinets containing priceless curiosities and of the little coquettish perfumed reception rooms made for chatting at five o'clock with intimate friends, with men famous and sought after, whom all women envy and whose attention they all desire.

When she sat down to dinner, before the round table covered with a tablecloth in use three days, opposite her husband, who uncovered the soup tureen and declared with a delighted air, "Ah, the good soup! I don't know anything better than that," she thought of dainty dinners, of shining silverware, of tapestry that peopled the walls with ancient personages and with strange birds flying in the midst of a fairy forest; and she thought of delicious dishes served on marvellous plates and of the whispered gallantries to which you listen with a sphinxlike smile while you are eating the pink meat of a trout or the wings of a quail.

She had no gowns, no jewels, nothing. And she loved nothing but that. She felt made for that. She would have liked so much to please, to be envied, to be charming, to be sought after.

She had a friend, a former schoolmate at the convent, who was rich, and whom she did not like to go to see any more because she felt so sad when she came home.

But one evening her husband reached home with a triumphant air and holding a large envelope in his hand.

"There," said he, "there is something for you."

She tore the paper quickly and drew out a printed card which bore these words:

The Minister of Public Instruction and Madame Georges Ramponneau request the honor of M. and Madame Loisel's company at the palace of the Ministry on Monday evening, January 18th.

Instead of being delighted, as her husband had hoped, she threw the invitation on the table crossly, muttering:

"What do you wish me to do with that?"

"Why, my dear, I thought you would be glad. You never go out, and this is such a fine opportunity. I had great trouble to get it. Every one wants to go; it is very select, and they are not giving many invitations to clerks. The whole official world will be there."

She looked at him with an irritated glance and said impatiently:

"And what do you wish me to put on my back?"

He had not thought of that. He stammered:

"Why, the gown you go to the theatre in. It looks very well to me."

He stopped, distracted, seeing that his wife was weeping. Two great tears ran slowly from the corners of her eyes toward the corners of her mouth.

"What's the matter? What's the matter?" he answered.

By a violent effort she conquered her grief and replied in a calm voice, while she wiped her wet cheeks:

"Nothing. Only I have no gown, and, therefore, I can't go to this ball. Give your card to some colleague whose wife is better equipped than I am."

He was in despair. He resumed:

"Come, let us see, Mathilde. How much would it cost, a suitable gown, which you could use on other occasions—something very simple?"

She reflected several seconds, making her calculations and wondering also what sum she could ask without drawing on herself an immediate refusal and a frightened exclamation from the economical clerk.

Finally she replied hesitating:

"I don't know exactly, but I think I could manage it with four hundred francs."

He grew a little pale, because he was laying aside just that amount to buy a gun and treat himself to a little shooting next summer on the plain of Nanterre, with several friends who went to shoot larks there of a Sunday.

But he said:

"Very well. I will give you four hundred francs. And try to have a pretty gown."

The day of the ball drew near and Madame Loisel seemed sad, uneasy, anxious. Her frock was ready, however. Her husband said to her one evening:

"What is the matter? Come, you have seemed very queer these last three days."

And she answered:

"It annoys me not to have a single piece of jewelry, not a single ornament, nothing to put on. I shall look poverty-stricken. I would almost rather not go at all."

"You might wear natural flowers," said her husband. "They're very stylish at this time of year. For ten francs you can get two or three magnificent roses."

She was not convinced.

"No; there's nothing more humiliating than to look poor among other women who are rich."

"How stupid you are!" her husband cried. "Go look up your friend, Madame Forestier, and ask her to lend you some jewels. You're intimate enough with her to do that."

She uttered a cry of joy:

"True! I never thought of it."

The next day she went to her friend and told her of her distress.

Madame Forestier went to a wardrobe with a mirror, took out a large jewel box, brought it back, opened it and said to Madame Loisel:

"Choose, my dear."

She saw first some bracelets, then a pearl

necklace, then a Venetian gold cross set with precious stones, of admirable workmanship. She tried on the ornaments before the mirror, hesitated and could not make up her mind to part with them, to give them back. She kept asking:

"Haven't you any more?"

"Why, yes. Look further; I don't know what you like."

Suddenly she discovered, in a black satin box, a superb diamond necklace, and her heart throbbed with an immoderate desire. Her hands trembled as she took it. She fastened it round her throat, outside her high-necked waist, and was lost in ecstasy at her reflection in the mirror.

Then she asked, hesitating, filled with anxious doubt:

"Will you lend me this, only this?"

"Why, yes, certainly."

She threw her arms round her friend's neck, kissed her passionately, then fled with her treasure.

The night of the ball arrived. Madame Loisel

was a great success. She was prettier than any other woman present, elegant, graceful, smiling and wild with joy. All the men looked at her, asked her name, sought to be introduced. All the attaches of the Cabinet wished to waltz with her. She was remarked by the minister himself.

She danced with rapture, with passion, intoxicated by pleasure, forgetting all in the triumph of her beauty, in the glory of her success, in a sort of cloud of happiness comprised of all this homage, admiration, these awakened desires and of that sense of triumph which is so sweet to woman's heart.

She left the ball about four o'clock in the morning. Her husband had been sleeping since midnight in a little deserted anteroom with three other gentlemen whose wives were enjoying the ball.

He threw over her shoulders the wraps he had brought, the modest wraps of common life, the poverty of which contrasted with the elegance of the ball dress. She felt this and wished to escape so as not to be remarked by the other women, who were enveloping themselves in costly furs.

Loisel held her back, saying: "Wait a bit. You will catch cold outside. I will call a cab."

But she did not listen to him and rapidly descended the stairs. When they reached the street they could not find a carriage and began to look for one, shouting after the cabmen passing at a distance.

They went toward the Seine in despair, shivering with cold. At last they found on the quay one of those ancient night cabs which, as though they were ashamed to show their shabbiness during the day, are never seen round Paris until after dark.

It took them to their dwelling in the Rue des Martyrs, and sadly they mounted the stairs to their flat. All was ended for her. As to him, he reflected that he must be at the ministry at ten o'clock that morning.

She removed her wraps before the glass so as to see herself once more in all her glory. But suddenly she uttered a cry. She no longer had the necklace around her neck!

"What is the matter with you?" demanded her husband, already half undressed.

She turned distractedly toward him.

"I have—I have—I've lost Madame Forestier's necklace," she cried.

He stood up, bewildered.

"What!—how? Impossible!"

They looked among the folds of her skirt, of her cloak, in her pockets, everywhere, but did not find it.

"You're sure you had it on when you left the ball?" he asked.

"Yes, I felt it in the vestibule of the minister's house."

"But if you had lost it in the street we should have heard it fall. It must be in the cab."

"Yes, probably. Did you take his number?"

"No. And you—didn't you notice it?"

"No."

They looked, thunderstruck, at each other. At last Loisel put on his clothes.

"I shall go back on foot," said he, "over the whole route, to see whether I can find it."

He went out. She sat waiting on a chair in her ball dress, without strength to go to bed, overwhelmed, without any fire, without a thought.

Her husband returned about seven o'clock. He had found nothing.

He went to police headquarters, to the newspaper offices to offer a reward; he went to the cab companies—everywhere, in fact, whither he was urged by the least spark of hope.

She waited all day, in the same condition of mad fear before this terrible calamity.

Loisel returned at night with a hollow, pale face. He had discovered nothing.

"You must write to your friend," said he, "that you have broken the clasp of her necklace and that you are having it mended. That will give us time to turn round."

She wrote at his dictation.

At the end of a week they had lost all hope.

Loisel, who had aged five years, declared:

"We must consider how to replace that ornament."

The next day they took the box that had contained it and went to the jeweler whose name was found within. He consulted his books.

"It was not I, madame, who sold that necklace; I must simply have furnished the case."

Then they went from jeweler to jeweler, searching for a necklace like the other, trying to recall it, both sick with chagrin and grief.

They found, in a shop at the Palais Royal, a string of diamonds that seemed to them exactly like the one they had lost. It was worth forty thousand francs. They could have it for thirty-six.

So they begged the jeweler not to sell it for three days yet. And they made a bargain that he should buy it back for thirty-four thousand francs, in case they should find the lost necklace before the end of February.

Loisel possessed eighteen thousand francs

which his father had left him. He would borrow the rest.

He did borrow, asking a thousand francs of one, five hundred of another, five louis here, three louis there. He gave notes, took up ruinous obligations, dealt with usurers and all the race of lenders. He compromised all the rest of his life, risked signing a note without even knowing whether he could meet it; and, frightened by the trouble yet to come, by the black misery that was about to fall upon him, by the prospect of all the physical privations and moral tortures that he was to suffer, he went to get the new necklace, laying upon the jeweler's counter thirty-six thousand francs.

When Madame Loisel took back the necklace Madame Forestier said to her with a chilly manner:

"You should have returned it sooner; I might have needed it."

She did not open the case, as her friend had so much feared. If she had detected the substitution, what would she have thought, what would she have said? Would she not have taken Madame Loisel for a thief?

Thereafter Madame Loisel knew the horrible existence of the needy. She bore her part, however, with sudden heroism. That dreadful debt must be paid. She would pay it. They dismissed their servant; they changed their lodgings; they rented a garret under the roof.

She came to know what heavy housework meant and the odious cares of the kitchen. She washed the dishes, using her dainty fingers and rosy nails on greasy pots and pans. She washed the soiled linen, the shirts and the dishcloths, which she dried upon a line; she carried the slops down to the street every morning and carried up the water, stopping for breath at every landing. And dressed like a woman of the people, she went to the fruiterer, the grocer, the butcher, a basket on her arm, bargaining, meeting with impertinence, defending her miserable money, sou by sou.

Every month they had to meet some notes, renew others, obtain more time.

Her husband worked evenings, making up a tradesman's accounts, and late at night he often copied manuscript for five sous a page.

This life lasted ten years.

At the end of ten years they had paid everything, everything, with the rates of usury and the accumulations of the compound interest.

Madame Loisel looked old now. She had become the woman of impoverished households—strong and hard and rough. With frowsy hair, skirts askew and red hands, she talked loud while washing the floor with great swishes of water. But sometimes, when her husband was at the office, she sat down near the window and she thought of that gay evening of long ago, of that ball where she had been so beautiful and so admired.

What would have happened if she had not lost that necklace? Who knows? who knows? How strange and changeful is life! How small a thing is needed to make or ruin us!

But one Sunday, having gone to take a walk in

the Champs Elysees to refresh herself after the labors of the week, she suddenly perceived a woman who was leading a child. It was Madame Forestier, still young, still beautiful, still charming.

Madame Loisel felt moved. Should she speak to her? Yes, certainly. And now that she had paid, she would tell her all about it. Why not?

She went up.

"Good-day, Jeanne."

The other, astonished to be familiarly addressed by this plain good-wife, did not recognize her at all and stammered:

"But—madame!—I do not know—You must have mistaken."

"No. I am Mathilde Loisel."

Her friend uttered a cry.

"Oh, my poor Mathilde! How you are changed!"

"Yes, I have had a pretty hard life, since I last saw you, and great poverty—and that because of you!"

"Of me! How so?"

"Do you remember that diamond necklace you lent me to wear at the ministerial ball?"

"Yes. Well?"

"Well, I lost it."

"What do you mean? You brought it back."

"I brought you back another exactly like it. And it has taken us ten years to pay for it. You can understand that it was not easy for us, for us who had nothing. At last it is ended, and I am very glad."

Madame Forestier had stopped.

"You say that you bought a necklace of diamonds to replace mine?"

"Yes. You never noticed it, then! They were very similar."

And she smiled with a joy that was at once proud and ingenuous.

Madame Forestier, deeply moved, took her hands.

"Oh, my poor Mathilde! Why, my necklace was paste! It was worth at most only five hundred francs!"

AN OCCURRENCE AT OWL CREEK BRIDGE

by Ambrose Bierce

I

A man stood upon a railroad bridge in northern Alabama, looking down into the swift water twenty feet below. The man's hands were behind his back, the wrists bound with a cord. A rope closely encircled his neck. It was attached to a stout cross-timber above his head and the slack fell to the level of his knees. Some loose boards laid upon the ties supporting the rails of the railway supplied a footing for him and his executioners—two private soldiers of the Federal army, directed by a sergeant who in civil life may have been a deputy sheriff. At a short remove upon the same temporary platform was an officer in the uniform of his rank, armed. He was a captain. A sentinel at each end of the bridge stood with his rifle in the position known as "support," that is to say, vertical in front of the left shoulder, the hammer resting on the forearm thrown straight across the chest—a formal and unnatural position, enforcing an erect carriage of the body. It did not appear to be the duty of these two men to know what was occurring at the center of the bridge; they merely blockaded the two ends of the foot planking that traversed it.

Beyond one of the sentinels nobody was in sight; the railroad ran straight away into a forest for a hundred yards, then, curving, was lost to view. Doubtless there was an outpost farther along. The other bank of the stream was open ground—a gentle slope topped with a stockade of vertical tree trunks, loopholed for rifles, with a single embrasure through which protruded the muzzle of a brass cannon commanding the bridge. Midway up the slope between the bridge and fort were the spectators—a single company of infantry in line, at "parade rest," the butts of their rifles on the ground, the barrels inclining slightly backward against the right shoulder, the hands crossed upon the stock. A lieutenant stood at the right of the line, the point of his sword upon the ground, his left hand resting upon his right. Excepting the group of four at the center of the bridge, not a man moved. The company faced the bridge, staring stonily, motionless. The sentinels, facing the banks of the stream, might have been statues to adorn the bridge. The captain stood with folded arms, silent, observing the work of his subordinates, but making no sign. Death is a dignitary who when he comes announced is to be received with formal manifestations of respect, even by those most familiar with him. In the code of military etiquette silence and fixity are forms of deference.

The man who was engaged in being hanged was apparently about thirty-five years of age. He was a civilian, if one might judge from his habit, which was that of a planter. His features were good—a straight nose, firm mouth, broad forehead, from which his long, dark hair was combed straight back, falling behind his ears to the collar of his well fitting frock coat. He wore a moustache and pointed beard, but no whiskers; his eyes were large and dark gray, and had a kindly expression which one would hardly have expected in one whose neck was in the hemp. Evidently this was no vulgar assassin. The liberal military code makes provision for hanging many kinds of persons, and gentlemen are not excluded.

The preparations being complete, the two private soldiers stepped aside and each drew away the plank upon which he had been standing. The sergeant turned to the captain, saluted and placed himself immediately behind that officer, who in turn moved apart one pace. These movements left the condemned man and the sergeant standing on the two ends of the same plank, which spanned three of the cross-ties of the bridge. The end upon which the civilian stood almost, but not quite, reached a fourth. This plank had been held in place by the weight of the captain; it was now held by that of the sergeant. At a signal from the former the latter would step aside, the plank would tilt and the condemned man go down between two ties. The arrangement commended itself to his judgement as simple and effective. His face had not been covered nor his eyes bandaged. He looked a moment at his "unsteadfast footing," then let his gaze wander to the swirling water of the stream racing madly beneath his feet. A piece of dancing driftwood caught his attention and his eyes followed it down the current. How slowly it appeared to move! What a sluggish stream!

He closed his eyes in order to fix his last thoughts upon his wife and children. The water, touched to gold by the early sun, the brooding mists under the banks at some distance down the stream, the fort, the soldiers, the piece of drift—all had distracted him. And now he became conscious of a new disturbance. Striking through the thought of his dear ones was sound which he could neither ignore nor understand, a sharp, distinct, metallic percussion like the stroke of a blacksmith's hammer upon the anvil; it had the same ringing quality. He wondered what it was, and whether immeasurably distant or near by—it seemed both. Its recurrence was regular, but as slow as the tolling of a death knell. He awaited each new stroke with impatience and—he knew not why—apprehension. The intervals of silence grew progressively longer; the delays became maddening. With their greater infrequency the sounds increased in strength and sharpness. They hurt his ear like the trust of a knife; he feared he would shriek. What he heard was the ticking of his watch.

He unclosed his eyes and saw again the water below him. "If I could free my hands," he thought, "I might throw off the noose and spring into the stream. By diving I could evade the bullets and, swimming vigorously, reach the bank, take to the woods and get away home. My home, thank God, is as yet outside their lines; my wife and little ones are still beyond the invader's farthest advance."

As these thoughts, which have here to be set down in words, were flashed into the doomed man's brain rather than evolved from it the captain nodded to the sergeant. The sergeant stepped aside.

II

Peyton Fahrquhar was a well to do planter, of an old and highly respected Alabama family. Being a slave owner and like other slave owners a politician, he was naturally an original secessionist and ardently devoted to the Southern cause. Circumstances of an imperious nature, which it is unnecessary to relate here, had prevented him from taking service with that gallant army which had fought the disastrous campaigns ending with the fall of Corinth, and he chafed under the inglorious restraint, longing for the release of his energies, the larger life of the soldier, the opportunity for distinction. That opportunity, he felt, would come, as it comes to all in wartime. Meanwhile he did what he could. No service was too humble for him to perform in the aid of the South, no adventure to perilous for him to undertake if consistent with the character of a civilian who was at heart a soldier, and who in good faith and without too much qualification assented to at least a part of the frankly villainous dictum that all is fair in love and war.

One evening while Fahrquhar and his wife were sitting on a rustic bench near the entrance to his grounds, a gray-clad soldier rode up to the gate and asked for a drink of water. Mrs. Fahrquhar was only too happy to serve him with her own white hands. While she was fetching the water her husband approached the dusty horseman and inquired eagerly for news from the front.

"The Yanks are repairing the railroads," said the man, "and are getting ready for another advance. They have reached the Owl Creek bridge, put it in order and built a stockade on the north bank. The commandant has issued an order, which is posted everywhere, declaring that any civilian caught interfering with the railroad, its bridges, tunnels, or trains will be summarily hanged. I saw the order."

"How far is it to the Owl Creek bridge?" Fahrquhar asked.

"About thirty miles."

"Is there no force on this side of the creek?"

"Only a picket post half a mile out, on the railroad, and a single sentinel at this end of the bridge."

"Suppose a man—a civilian and student of hanging—should elude the picket post and perhaps get the better of the sentinel," said Fahrquhar, smiling, "what could he accomplish?"

The soldier reflected. "I was there a month ago," he replied. "I observed that the flood of last winter had lodged a great quantity of driftwood against the wooden pier at this end of the bridge. It is now dry and would burn like tinder."

The lady had now brought the water, which the soldier drank. He thanked her ceremoniously, bowed to her husband and rode away. An hour later, after nightfall, he repassed the plantation, going northward in the direction from which he had come. He was a Federal scout.

III

As Peyton Fahrquhar fell straight downward through the bridge he lost consciousness and was as one already dead. From this state he was awakened—ages later, it seemed to him—by the pain of a sharp pressure upon his throat, followed by a sense of suffocation. Keen, poignant agonies seemed to shoot from his neck downward through every fiber of his body and limbs. These pains appeared to flash along well defined lines of ramification and to beat with an inconceivably rapid periodicity. They seemed like streams of pulsating fire heating him to an intolerable temperature. As to his head, he was conscious of nothing but a feeling of fullness—of congestion. These sensations were unaccompanied by thought. The intellectual part of his nature was already effaced; he had power only to feel, and feeling was torment. He was conscious of motion. Encompassed in a luminous cloud, of which he was now merely the fiery heart, without material substance, he swung through unthinkable arcs of oscillation, like a vast pendulum. Then all at once, with terrible suddenness, the light about him shot upward with the noise of a loud splash; a frightful roaring was in his ears, and all was cold and dark. The power of thought was restored; he knew that the rope had broken and he had fallen into the stream. There was no additional strangulation; the noose about his neck was already suffocating him and kept the water from his lungs. To die of hanging at the bottom of a river!—the idea seemed to him ludicrous. He opened his eyes in the darkness and saw above him a gleam of light, but how distant, how inaccessible! He was still sinking, for the light became fainter and fainter until it was a mere glimmer. Then it began to grow and brighten, and he knew that he was rising toward the surface—knew it with reluctance, for he was now very comfortable. "To be hanged and drowned," he thought, "that is not so bad; but I do not wish to be shot. No; I will not be shot; that is not fair."

He was not conscious of an effort, but a sharp

pain in his wrist apprised him that he was trying to free his hands. He gave the struggle his attention, as an idler might observe the feat of a juggler, without interest in the outcome. What splendid effort!—what magnificent, what superhuman strength! Ah, that was a fine endeavor! Bravo! The cord fell away; his arms parted and floated upward, the hands dimly seen on each side in the growing light. He watched them with a new interest as first one and then the other pounced upon the noose at his neck. They tore it away and thrust it fiercely aside, its undulations resembling those of a water snake. "Put it back, put it back!" He thought he shouted these words to his hands, for the undoing of the noose had been succeeded by the direst pang that he had yet experienced. His neck ached horribly; his brain was on fire, his heart, which had been fluttering faintly, gave a great leap, trying to force itself out at his mouth. His whole body was racked and wrenched with an insupportable anguish! But his disobedient hands gave no heed to the command. They beat the water vigorously with quick, downward strokes, forcing him to the surface. He felt his head emerge; his eyes were blinded by the sunlight; his chest expanded convulsively, and with a supreme and crowning agony his lungs engulfed a great draught of air, which instantly he expelled in a shriek!

He was now in full possession of his physical senses. They were, indeed, preternaturally keen and alert. Something in the awful disturbance of his organic system had so exalted and refined them that they made record of things never before perceived. He felt the ripples upon his face and heard their separate sounds as they struck. He looked at the forest on the bank of the stream, saw the individual trees, the leaves and the veining of each leaf—he saw the very insects upon them: the locusts, the brilliant bodied flies, the gray spiders stretching their webs from twig to twig. He noted the prismatic colors in all the dewdrops upon a million blades of grass. The humming of the gnats that danced above the eddies of the stream, the beating of the dragon flies' wings, the strokes of the water spiders' legs, like oars which had lifted their boat—all these made audible music. A fish slid along beneath his eyes and he heard the rush of its body parting the water.

He had come to the surface facing down the stream; in a moment the visible world seemed to wheel slowly round, himself the pivotal point, and he saw the bridge, the fort, the soldiers upon the bridge, the captain, the sergeant, the two privates, his executioners. They were in silhouette against the blue sky. They shouted and gesticulated, pointing at him. The captain had drawn his pistol, but did not fire; the others were unarmed. Their movements were grotesque and horrible, their forms gigantic.

Suddenly he heard a sharp report and something struck the water smartly within a few inches of his head, spattering his face with spray. He heard a second report, and saw one of the sentinels with his rifle at his shoulder, a light cloud of blue smoke rising from the muzzle. The man in the water saw the eye of the man on the bridge gazing into his own through the sights of the rifle. He observed that it was a gray eye and remembered having read that gray eyes were keenest, and that all famous marksmen had them.

Nevertheless, this one had missed.

A counter-swirl had caught Fahrquhar and turned him half round; he was again looking at the forest on the bank opposite the fort. The sound of a clear, high voice in a monotonous singsong now rang out behind him and came across the water with a distinctness that pierced and subdued all other sounds, even the beating of the ripples in his ears. Although no soldier, he had frequented camps enough to know the dread significance of that deliberate, drawling, aspirated chant; the lieutenant on shore was taking a part in the morning's work. How coldly and pitilessly—with what an even, calm intonation, presaging, and enforcing tranquility in the men—with what accurately measured interval fell those cruel words:

"Company! . . . Attention! . . . Shoulder arms! . . . Ready! . . . Aim! . . . Fire!"

Fahrquhar dived—dived as deeply as he could. The water roared in his ears like the voice of Niagara, yet he heard the dull thunder of the volley and, rising again toward the surface, met shining bits of metal, singularly flattened, oscillating slowly downward. Some of them touched him on the face and hands, then fell away, continuing their descent. One lodged between his collar and neck; it was uncomfortably warm and he snatched it out.

As he rose to the surface, gasping for breath, he saw that he had been a long time under water; he was perceptibly farther downstream—nearer to safety. The soldiers had almost finished reloading; the metal ramrods flashed all at once in the sunshine as they were drawn from the barrels, turned in the air, and thrust into their sockets. The two sentinels fired again, independently and ineffectually.

The hunted man saw all this over his shoulder; he was now swimming vigorously with the current. His brain was as energetic as his arms and legs; he thought with the rapidity of lightning:

"The officer," he reasoned, "will not make that martinet's error a second time. It is as easy to dodge a volley as a single shot. He has probably already given the command to fire at will. God help me, I cannot dodge them all!"

An appalling splash within two yards of him was followed by a loud, rushing sound, *diminuendo*, which seemed to travel back through the air to the fort and died in an explosion which stirred the very river to its deeps! A rising sheet of water curved over him, fell down upon him, blinded him, strangled him! The cannon had taken an hand in the game. As he shook his head free from the commotion of the smitten water he heard the deflected shot humming through the air ahead, and in an instant it was cracking and smashing the branches in the forest beyond.

"They will not do that again," he thought; "the next time they will use a charge of grape. I must keep my eye upon the gun; the smoke will apprise me —the report arrives too late; it lags behind the missile. That is a good gun."

Suddenly he felt himself whirled round and round—spinning like a top. The water, the banks, the forests, the now distant bridge, fort and men, all were commingled and blurred. Objects were represented by their colors only; circular horizontal streaks of color—that was all he saw. He had been caught in a vortex and was being whirled on with a velocity of advance and gyration that made him giddy and sick. In few moments he was flung upon the gravel at the foot of the left bank of the stream—the southern bank—and behind a projecting point which concealed him from his enemies. The sudden arrest of his motion, the abrasion of one of his hands on the gravel, restored him, and he wept with delight. He dug his fingers into the sand, threw it over himself in handfuls and audibly blessed it. It looked like diamonds, rubies, emeralds; he could think of nothing beautiful which it did not resemble. The trees upon the bank were giant garden plants; he noted a definite order in their arrangement, inhaled the fragrance of their blooms. A strange roseate light shone through the spaces among their trunks and the wind made in their branches the music of Aeolian harps. He had not wish to perfect his escape—he was content to remain in that enchanting spot until retaken.

A whiz and a rattle of grapeshot among the branches high above his head roused him from his dream. The baffled cannoneer had fired him a random farewell. He sprang to his feet, rushed up the sloping bank, and plunged into the forest.

All that day he traveled, laying his course by the rounding sun. The forest seemed interminable; nowhere did he discover a break in it, not even a woodman's road. He had not known that he lived in so wild a region. There was something uncanny in the revelation.

By nightfall he was fatigued, footsore, famished. The thought of his wife and children urged him on. At last he found a road which led him in what he knew to be the right direction. It was as wide and straight as a city street, yet it seemed untraveled. No fields bordered it, no dwelling anywhere. Not so much as the barking of a dog suggested human habitation. The black bodies of the trees formed a straight wall on both sides, terminating on the horizon in a point, like a diagram in a lesson in perspective. Overhead, as he looked up through this rift in the wood, shone great golden stars looking unfamiliar and grouped in strange constellations. He was sure they were arranged in some order which had a secret and malign significance. The wood on either side was full of singular noises, among which—once, twice, and again—he distinctly heard whispers in an unknown tongue.

His neck was in pain and lifting his hand to it found it horribly swollen. He knew that it had a circle of black where the rope had bruised it. His eyes felt congested; he could no longer close them. His tongue was swollen with thirst; he relieved its fever by thrusting it forward from between his teeth into the cold air. How softly the turf had carpeted the untraveled avenue—he could no longer feel the roadway beneath his feet!

Doubtless, despite his suffering, he had fallen

asleep while walking, for now he sees another scene—perhaps he has merely recovered from a delirium. He stands at the gate of his own home. All is as he left it, and all bright and beautiful in the morning sunshine. He must have traveled the entire night. As he pushes open the gate and passes up the wide white walk, he sees a flutter of female garments; his wife, looking fresh and cool and sweet, steps down from the veranda to meet him. At the bottom of the steps she stands waiting, with a smile of ineffable joy, an attitude of matchless grace and dignity. Ah, how beautiful she is! He springs forwards with extended arms. As he is about to clasp her he feels a stunning blow upon the back of the neck; a blinding white light blazes all about him with a sound like the shock of a cannon—then all is darkness and silence!

Peyton Fahrquhar was dead; his body, with a broken neck, swung gently from side to side beneath the timbers of the Owl Creek bridge.

THE CASE OF LADY SANNOX

by Sir Arthur Conan Doyle

The relations between Douglas Stone and the notorious Lady Sannox were very well known both among the fashionable circles of which she was a brilliant member, and the scientific bodies which numbered him among their most illustrious confreres. There was naturally, therefore, a very widespread interest when it was announced one morning that the lady had absolutely and for ever taken the veil, and that the world would see her no more. When, at the very tail of this rumour, there came the assurance that the celebrated operating surgeon, the man of steel nerves, had been found in the morning by his valet, seated on one side of his bed, smiling pleasantly upon the universe, with both legs jammed into one side of his breeches and his great brain about as valuable as a cap full of porridge, the matter was strong enough to give quite a little thrill of interest to folk who had never hoped that their jaded nerves were capable of such a sensation.

Douglas Stone in his prime was one of the most remarkable men in England. Indeed, he could hardly be said to have ever reached his prime, for he was but nine-and-thirty at the time of this little incident. Those who knew him best were aware that famous as he was as a surgeon, he might have succeeded with even greater rapidity in any of a dozen lines of life. He could have cut his way to fame as a soldier, struggled to it as an explorer, bullied for it in the courts, or built it out of stone and iron as an engineer. He was born to be great, for he could plan what another man dare not do, and he could do what another man dare not plan. In surgery none could follow him. His nerve, his judgement, his intuition, were things apart. Again and again his knife cut away death, but grazed the very springs of life in doing it, until his assistants were as white as the patient. His energy, his audacity, his full-blooded self-confidence -

does not the memory of them still linger to the south of Marylebone Road and the north of Oxford Street?

His vices were as magnificent as his virtues, and infinitely more picturesque. Large as was his income, and it was the third largest of all professional men in London, it was far beneath the luxury of his living. Deep in his complex nature lay a rich vein of sensualism, at the sport of which he placed all the prizes of his life. The eye, the ear, the touch, the palate, all were his masters. The bouquet of old vintages, the scent of rare exotics, the curves and tints of the daintiest potteries of Europe, it was to these that the quick-running stream of gold was transformed. And then there came his sudden mad passion for Lady Sannox, when a single interview with two challenging glances and a whispered word set him ablaze. She was the loveliest woman in London and the only one to him. He was one of the handsomest men in London, but not the only one to her. She had a liking for new experiences, and was gracious to most men who wooed her. It may have been cause or it may have been effect that Lord Sannox looked fifty, though he was but six-and-thirty.

He was a quiet, silent, neutral-tinted man, this lord, with thin lips and heavy eyelids, much given to gardening, and full of home-like habits. He had at one time been fond of acting, had even rented a theatre in London, and on its boards had first seen Miss Marion Dawson, to whom he had offered his hand, his title, and the third of a county. Since his marriage his early hobby had become distasteful to him. Even in private theatricals it was no longer possible to persuade him to exercise the talent which he had often showed that he possessed. He was happier with a spud and a watering-can among his orchids and chrysanthemums.

It was quite an interesting problem whether he was absolutely devoid of sense, or miserably wanting in spirit. Did he know his lady's ways and condone them, or was he a mere blind, doting fool? It was a point to be discussed over the teacups in snug little drawing-rooms, or with the aid of a cigar in the bow windows of clubs. Bitter and plain were the comments among men upon his conduct. There was but one who had a good word to say for him, and he was the most silent member in the smoking-room. He had seen him break in a horse at the University, and it seemed to have left an impression upon his mind.

But when Douglas Stone became the favourite all doubts as to Lord Sannox's knowledge or ignorance were set for ever at rest. There was no subterfuge about Stone. In his high-handed, impetuous fashion, he set all caution and discretion at defiance. The scandal became notorious. A learned body intimated that his name had been struck from the list of its vice-presidents. Two friends implored him to consider his professional credit. He cursed them all three, and spent forty guineas on a bangle to take with him to the lady. He was at her house every evening, and she drove in his carriage in the afternoons. There was not an attempt on either side to conceal their relations; but there came at last a little incident to interrupt them.

It was a dismal winter's night, very cold and gusty, with the wind whooping in the chimneys and blustering against the window-panes. A thin spatter of rain tinkled on the glass with each fresh sough of the gale, drowning for the instant the dull gurgle and drip from the eaves. Douglas Stone had finished his dinner, and sat by his fire in the study, a glass of rich port upon the malachite table at his elbow. As he raised it to his lips, he held it up against the lamplight, and watched with the eye of a connoisseur the tiny scales of beeswing which floated in its rich ruby depths. The fire, as it spurted up, threw fitful lights upon his bald, clear-cut face, with its widely-opened grey eyes, its thick and yet firm lips, and the deep, square jaw, which had something Roman in its strength and its animalism. He smiled from time to time as he nestled back in his luxurious chair. Indeed, he had a right to feel well pleased, for, against the advice of six colleagues, he had performed an operation that day of which only two cases were on record, and the result had been brilliant beyond all expectation. No other man in London would have had the daring to plan, or the skill to execute, such a heroic measure.

But he had promised Lady Sannox to see her that evening and it was already half-past eight. His hand was outstretched to the bell to order the carriage when he heard the dull thud of the knocker. An instant later there was the shuffling of feet in the hall, and the sharp closing of a door.

"A patient to see you, sir, in the consulting room," said the butler.

"About himself?"

"No, sir; I think he wants you to go out."

"It is too late," cried Douglas Stone peevishly. "I won't go."

"This is his card, sir."

The butler presented it upon the gold salver which had been given to his master by the wife of a Prime Minister.

"'Hamil Ali, Smyrna.' Hum! The fellow is a

Turk, I suppose."

"Yes, sir. He seems as if he came from abroad, sir. And he's in a terrible way."

"Tut, tut! I have an engagement. I must go somewhere else. But I'll see him. Show him in here, Pim."

A few moments later the butler swung open the door and ushered in a small and decrepit man, who walked with a bent back and with the forward push of the face and blink of the eyes which goes with extreme short sight. His face was swarthy, and his hair and beard of the deepest black. In one hand he held a turban of white muslin striped with red, in the other a small chamois-leather bag.

"Good evening," said Douglas Stone, when the butler had closed the door. "You speak English, I presume?"

"Yes, sir. I am from Asia Minor, but I speak English when I speak slow."

"You wanted me to go out, I understand?"

"Yes, sir. I wanted very much that you should see my wife."

"I could come in the morning, but I have an engagement which prevents me from seeing your wife tonight."

The Turk's answer was a singular one. He pulled the string which closed the mouth of the chamois-leather bag, and poured a flood of gold on to the table.

"There are one hundred pounds there," said he, "and I promise you that it will not take you an hour. I have a cab ready at the door."

Douglas Stone glanced at his watch. An hour would not make it too late to visit Lady Sannox. He had been there later. And the fee was an extraordinarily high one. He had been pressed by his creditors lately, and he could not afford to let such a chance pass. He would go.

"What is the case?" he asked.

"Oh, it is so sad a one! So sad a one! You have not, perhaps heard of the daggers of the Almohades?"

"Never."

"Ah, they are Eastern daggers of a great age and of a singular shape, with the hilt like what you call a stirrup. I am a curiosity dealer, you understand, and that is why I have come to England from Smyrna, but next week I go back once more. Many things I brought with me, and I have a few things left, but among them, to my sorrow, is one of these daggers."

"You will remember that I have an appointment, sir," said the surgeon, with some irritation; "pray confine yourself to the necessary details."

"You will see that it is necessary. Today my wife fell down in a faint in the room in which I keep my wares, and she cut her lower lip upon this cursed dagger of Almohades."

"I see," said Douglas Stone, rising. "And you wish me to dress the wound?"

"No, no, it is worse than that."

"What then?"

"These daggers are poisoned."

"Poisoned!"

"Yes, and there is no man, East or West, who can tell now what is the poison or what the cure. But all that is known I know, for my father was in this trade before me, and we have had much to do with these poisoned weapons."

"What are the symptoms?"

"Deep sleep, and death in thirty hours."

"And you say there is no cure. Why then should you pay me this considerable fee?"

"No drug can cure, but the knife may."

"And how?"

"The poison is slow of absorption. It remains

for hours in the wound."

"Washing, then, might cleanse it?"

"No more than in a snake bite. It is too subtle and too deadly."

"Excision of the wound, then?"

"That is it. If it be on the finger, take the finger off. So said my father always. But think of where this wound is, and that it is my wife. It is dreadful!"

But familiarity with such grim matters may take the finer edge from a man's sympathy. To Douglas Stone this was already an interesting case, and he brushed aside as irrelevant the feeble objections of the husband.

"It appears to be that or nothing," said he brusquely. "It is better to loose a lip than a life."

"Ah, yes, I know that you are right. Well, well, it is kismet, and it must be faced. I have the cab, and you will come with me and do this thing."

Douglas Stone took his case of bistouries from a drawer, and placed it with a roll of bandage and a compress of lint in his pocket. He must waste no more time if he were to see Lady Sannox.

"I am ready," said he, pulling on his overcoat. "Will you take a glass of wine before you go out into this cold air?"

His visitor shrank away, with a protesting hand upraised.

"You forget that I am a Mussulman, and a true follower of the Prophet," said he. "But tell me what is the bottle of green glass which you have placed in your pocket?"

"It is chloroform."

"Ah, that also is forbidden to us. It is a spirit, and we make no use of such things."

"What! You would allow your wife to go through an operation without an anaesthetic?"

"Ah! she will feel nothing, poor soul. The deep

sleep has already come on, which is the first working of the poison. And then I have given her of our Smyrna opium. Come, sir, for already an hour has passed."

As they stepped out into the darkness, a sheet of rain was driven in upon their faces, and the hall lamp, which dangled from the arm of a marble Caryatid, went out with a fluff. Pim, the butler, pushed the heavy door to, straining hard with his shoulder against the wind, while the two men groped their way towards the yellow glare which showed where the cab was waiting. An instant later they were rattling upon their journey.

"Is it far?" asked Douglas Stone.

"Oh, no. We have a very little quiet place off the Euston Road."

The surgeon pressed the spring of his repeater and listened to the little tings which told him the hour. It was a quarter past nine. He calculated the distances, and the short time which it would take him to perform so trivial an operation. He ought to reach Lady Sannox by ten o'clock. Through the fogged windows he saw the blurred gas lamps dancing past, with occasionally the broader glare of a shop front. The rain was pelting and rattling upon the leathern top of the carriage, and the wheels swashed as they rolled through puddle and mud. Opposite to him the white headgear of his companion gleamed faintly through the obscurity. The surgeon felt in his pockets and arranged his needles, his ligatures and his safety-pins, that no time might be wasted when they arrived. He chafed with impatience and drummed his foot upon the floor.

But the cab slowed down at last and pulled up. In an instant Douglas Stone was out, and the Smyrna merchant's toe was at his very heel.

"You can wait," said he to the driver.

It was a mean-looking house in a narrow and sordid street. The surgeon, who knew his London well, cast a swift glance into the shadows, but there was nothing distinctive - no shop, no movement, nothing but a double line of dull, flat-faced houses, a double stretch of wet flagstones which gleamed in the lamplight, and a double rush of water in the gutters which swirled and gurgled towards the sewer gratings. The door which faced them was blotched and discoloured, and a faint light in the fan pane above, it served to show the dust and the grime which covered it. Above in one of the bedroom windows, there was a dull yellow glimmer. The merchant knocked loudly, and, as he turned his dark face towards the light, Douglas Stone could see that it was contracted with anxiety. A bolt was drawn, and an elderly woman with a taper stood in the doorway, shielding the thin flame with her gnarled hand.

"Is all well?" gasped the merchant.

"She is as you left her, sir."

"She has not spoken?"

"No, she is in a deep sleep."

The merchant closed the door, and Douglas

Stone walked down the narrow passage, glancing about him in some surprise as he did so. There was no oil-cloth, no mat, no hat-rack. Deep grey dust and heavy festoons of cobwebs met his eyes everywhere. Following the old woman up the winding stair, his firm footfall echoed harshly through the silent house. There was no carpet.

The bedroom was on the second landing. Douglas Stone followed the old nurse into it, with the merchant at his heels. Here, at least, there was furniture and to spare. The floor was littered and the corners piled with Turkish cabinets, inlaid tables, coats of chain mail, strange pipes, and grotesque weapons. A single small lamp stood upon a bracket on the wall. Douglas Stone took it down, and picking his way among the lumber, walked over to a couch in the corner, on which lay a woman dressed in the Turkish fashion, with yashmak and veil. The lower part of the face was exposed, and the surgeon saw a jagged cut which zigzagged along the border of the under lip.

"You will forgive the yashmak," said the Turk.

"You know our views about women in the East."

But the surgeon was not thinking about the yashmak. This was no longer a woman to him. It was a case. He stooped and examined the wound carefully.

"There are no signs of irritation," said he. "We might delay the operation until local symptoms develop."

The husband wrung his hands in uncontrollable agitation.

"Oh! sir, sir," he cried. "Do not trifle. You do not know. It is deadly. I know, and I give you my assurance that an operation is absolutely necessary. Only the knife can save her."

"And yet I am inclined to wait," said Douglas Stone.

"That is enough," the Turk cried, angrily. "Every minute is of importance, and I cannot stand here and see my wife allowed to sink. It only remains for me to give you my thanks for having come, and to call in some other surgeon before it is too late."

Douglas Stone hesitated. To refund that hundred pounds was no pleasant matter. But of course if he left the case he must return the money. And if the Turk were right and the woman died, his position before a coroner might be an embarrassing one.

"You have had personal experience of this poison?" he asked.

"I have."

"And you assure me that an operation is needful."

"I swear it by all that I hold sacred."

"The disfigurement will be frightful."

"I can understand that the mouth will not be a pretty one to kiss."

Douglas Stone turned fiercely upon the man. The speech was a brutal one. But the Turk has his own fashion of talk and of thought, and there was no time for wrangling. Douglas Stone drew a bistoury from his case, opened it and felt the keen straight edge with his forefinger. Then he held the lamp closer to the bed. Two dark eyes were gazing up at him through the slit in the yashmak. They were all iris, and the pupil was hardly to be seen.

"You have given her a very heavy dose of opium."

"Yes, she has had a good dose."

He glanced again at the dark eyes which looked straight at his own. They were dull and lustreless, but, even as he gazed, a little shifting sparkle came into them, and the lips quivered.

"She is not absolutely unconscious," said he.

"Would it not be well to use the knife while it will be painless?"

The same thought had crossed the surgeon's mind. He grasped the wounded lip with his forceps, and with two swift cuts he took out a broad V-shaped piece. The woman sprang up on the couch with a dreadful gurgling scream. Her covering was torn from her face. It was a face that he knew. In spite of that protruding upper lip and that slobber of blood, it was a face that he knew. She kept on putting her hand up to the gap and screaming. Douglas Stone sat down at the foot of the couch with his knife and his forceps. The room was whirling round, and he had felt something go like a ripping seam behind his ear. A bystander would have said that his face was the more ghastly of the two. As in a dream, or as if he had been looking at something at the play, he was conscious that the Turk's hair and beard lay upon the table, and that Lord Sannox was leaning against the wall with his hand to his side, laughing silently. The screams had died away now, and the dreadful head had dropped back again upon the pillow, but Douglas Stone still sat motionless, and Lord Sannox still chuckled quietly to himself.

"It was really very necessary for Marion, this operation," said he, "not physically, but morally, you know, morally."

Douglas Stone stooped for yards and began to play with the fringe of the coverlet. His knife tinkled down upon the ground, but he still held the forceps and something more.

"I had long intended to make a little example," said Lord Sannox, suavely. "Your note of Wednesday miscarried, and I have it here in my pocket-book. I took some pains in carrying out my idea. The wound, by the way, was from nothing more dangerous than my signet ring."

He glanced keenly at his silent companion, and cocked the small revolver which he held in his coat pocket. But Douglas Stone was still picking at the coverlet.

"You see you have kept your appointment after all," said Lord Sannox.

And at that Douglas Stone began to laugh. He laughed long and loudly. But Lord Sannox did not laugh now. Something like fear sharpened and hardened his features. He walked from the room, and he walked on tiptoe. The old woman was waiting outside.

"Attend to your mistress when she awakes," said Lord Sannox.

Then he went down to the street. The cab was at the door, and the driver raised his hand to his hat.

"John," said Lord Sannox, "you will take the doctor home first. He will want leading downstairs, I think. Tell his butler that he has been taken ill at a case."

"Very good, sir."

"Then you can take Lady Sannox home."

"And how about yourself, sir?"

"Oh, my address for the next few months will be Hotel di Roma, Venice. Just see that the letters are sent on. And tell Stevens to exhibit all the purple chrysanthemums next Monday, and to wire me the result."

THE MONKEY'S PAW

by W. W. Jacobs

I

Without, the night was cold and wet, but in the small parlour of Laburnam Villa the blinds were drawn and the fire burned brightly. Father and son were at chess, the former, who possessed ideas about the game involving radical changes, putting his king into such sharp and unnecessary perils that it even provoked comment from the white-haired old lady knitting placidly by the fire.

"Hark at the wind," said Mr. White, who, having seen a fatal mistake after it was too late, was amiably desirous of preventing his son from seeing it.

"I'm listening," said the latter, grimly surveying the board as he stretched out his hand. "Check."

"I should hardly think that he'd come to-night," said his father, with his hand poised over the board.

"Mate," replied the son.

"That's the worst of living so far out," bawled Mr. White, with sudden and unlooked-for violence; "of all the beastly, slushy, out-of-the-way places to live in, this is the worst. Pathway's a bog, and the road's a torrent. I don't know what people are thinking about. I suppose because only two houses in the road are let, they think it doesn't matter."

"Never mind, dear," said his wife, soothingly; "perhaps you'll win the next one."

Mr. White looked up sharply, just in time to intercept a knowing glance between mother and son. The words died away on his lips, and he hid a guilty grin in his thin grey beard.

"There he is," said Herbert White, as the gate banged to loudly and heavy footsteps came toward the door.

The old man rose with hospitable haste, and

opening the door, was heard condoling with the new arrival. The new arrival also condoled with himself, so that Mrs. White said, "Tut, tut!" and coughed gently as her husband entered the room, followed by a tall, burly man, beady of eye and rubicund of visage.

"Sergeant-Major Morris," he said, introducing him.

The sergeant-major shook hands, and taking the proffered seat by the fire, watched contentedly while his host got out whiskey and tumblers and stood a small copper kettle on the fire.

At the third glass his eyes got brighter, and he began to talk, the little family circle regarding with eager interest this visitor from distant parts, as he squared his broad shoulders in the chair and spoke of wild scenes and doughty deeds; of wars and plagues and strange peoples.

"Twenty-one years of it," said Mr. White, nodding at his wife and son. "When he went away he was a slip of a youth in the warehouse. Now look at him."

"He don't look to have taken much harm," said Mrs. White, politely.

"I'd like to go to India myself," said the old man, "just to look round a bit, you know."

"Better where you are," said the sergeant-major, shaking his head. He put down the empty glass, and sighing softly, shook it again.

"I should like to see those old temples and fakirs and jugglers," said the old man. "What was that you started telling me the other day about a monkey's paw or something, Morris?"

"Nothing," said the soldier, hastily. "Leastways nothing worth hearing."

"Monkey's paw?" said Mrs. White, curiously.

"Well, it's just a bit of what you might call magic, perhaps," said the sergeant-major, offhandedly.

His three listeners leaned forward eagerly. The visitor absent-mindedly put his empty glass to his lips and then set it down again. His host filled it for him.

"To look at," said the sergeant-major, fumbling in his pocket, "it's just an ordinary little paw, dried to a mummy."

He took something out of his pocket and proffered it. Mrs. White drew back with a grimace, but her son, taking it, examined it curiously.

"And what is there special about it?" inquired Mr. White as he took it from his son, and having examined it, placed it upon the table.

"It had a spell put on it by an old fakir," said the sergeant-major, "a very holy man. He wanted to show that fate ruled people's lives, and that those who interfered with it did so to their sorrow. He put a spell on it so that three separate men could each have three wishes from it."

His manner was so impressive that his hearers were conscious that their light laughter jarred somewhat.

"Well, why don't you have three, sir?" said Herbert White, cleverly.

The soldier regarded him in the way that middle age is wont to regard presumptuous youth. "I have," he said, quietly, and his blotchy face whitened.

"And did you really have the three wishes granted?" asked Mrs. White.

"I did," said the sergeant-major, and his glass tapped against his strong teeth.

"And has anybody else wished?" persisted the old lady.

"The first man had his three wishes. Yes," was the reply; "I don't know what the first two were, but the third was for death. That's how I got the paw."

His tones were so grave that a hush fell upon the group.

"If you've had your three wishes, it's no good to you now, then, Morris," said the old man at last. "What do you keep it for?"

The soldier shook his head. "Fancy, I suppose," he said, slowly. "I did have some idea of selling it, but I don't think I will. It has caused enough mischief already. Besides, people won't buy. They think it's a fairy tale; some of them, and those who do think anything of it want to try it first and pay me afterward."

"If you could have another three wishes," said the old man, eyeing him keenly, "would you have them?"

"I don't know," said the other. "I don't know."

He took the paw, and dangling it between his forefinger and thumb, suddenly threw it upon the fire. White, with a slight cry, stooped down and snatched it off.

"Better let it burn," said the soldier, solemnly.

"If you don't want it, Morris," said the other, "give it to me."

"I won't," said his friend, doggedly. "I threw it on the fire. If you keep it, don't blame me for what happens. Pitch it on the fire again like a sensible man."

The other shook his head and examined his new possession closely. "How do you do it?" he inquired.

"Hold it up in your right hand and wish aloud," said the sergeant-major, "but I warn you of the consequences."

"Sounds like the Arabian Nights," said Mrs.

White, as she rose and began to set the supper. "Don't you think you might wish for four pairs of
hands for me?"

Her husband drew the talisman from pocket, and then all three burst into laughter as the sergeant-major, with a look of alarm on his face, caught him by the arm.

"If you must wish," he said, gruffly, "wish for something sensible."

Mr. White dropped it back in his pocket, and placing chairs, motioned his friend to the table. In the business of supper the talisman was partly forgotten, and afterward the three sat listening in an enthralled fashion to a second instalment of the soldier's adventures in India.

"If the tale about the monkey's paw is not more truthful than those he has been telling us," said Herbert, as the door closed behind their guest, just in time for him to catch the last train, "we sha'nt make much out of it."

"Did you give him anything for it, father?"

inquired Mrs. White, regarding her husband closely.

"A trifle," said he, colouring slightly. "He didn't want it, but I made him take it. And he pressed me again to throw it away."

"Likely," said Herbert, with pretended horror. "Why, we're going to be rich, and famous and happy. Wish to be an emperor, father, to begin with; then you can't be henpecked."

He darted round the table, pursued by the maligned Mrs. White armed with an antimacassar.

Mr. White took the paw from his pocket and eyed it dubiously. "I don't know what to wish for, and that's a fact," he said, slowly. "It seems to me I've got all I want."

"If you only cleared the house, you'd be quite happy, wouldn't you?" said Herbert, with his hand on his shoulder. "Well, wish for two hundred pounds, then; that 'll just do it."

His father, smiling shamefacedly at his own credulity, held up the talisman, as his son, with a solemn face, somewhat marred by a wink at his mother, sat down at the piano and struck a few impressive chords.

"I wish for two hundred pounds," said the old man distinctly.

A fine crash from the piano greeted the words, interrupted by a shuddering cry from the old man. His wife and son ran toward him.

"It moved," he cried, with a glance of disgust at the object as it lay on the floor.

"As I wished, it twisted in my hand like a snake."

"Well, I don't see the money," said his son as he picked it up and placed it on the table, "and I bet I never shall."

"It must have been your fancy, father," said his wife, regarding him anxiously.

He shook his head. "Never mind, though; there's no harm done, but it gave me a shock all the same."

They sat down by the fire again while the two men finished their pipes. Outside, the wind was higher than ever, and the old man started nervously at the sound of a door banging upstairs. A silence unusual and depressing settled upon all three, which lasted until the old couple rose to retire for the night.

"I expect you'll find the cash tied up in a big bag in the middle of your bed," said Herbert, as he bade them good-night, "and something horrible squatting up on top of the wardrobe watching you as you pocket your ill-gotten gains."

He sat alone in the darkness, gazing at the dying fire, and seeing faces in it. The last face was so horrible and so simian that he gazed at it in amazement.' It got so vivid that, with a little uneasy laugh, he felt on the table for a glass containing a little water to throw over it. His hand grasped the monkey's paw, and with a little shiver he wiped his hand on his coat and went up to bed.

II

In the brightness of the wintry sun next morning as it streamed over the breakfast table he laughed at his fears. There was an air of prosaic wholesomeness about the room which it had lacked on the previous night, and the dirty, shrivelled little paw was pitched on the sideboard with a carelessness which betokened no great belief in its virtues.

"I suppose all old soldiers are the same," said Mrs. White. "The idea of our listening to such nonsense! How could wishes be granted in these days? And if they could, how could two hundred pounds hurt you, father?"

"Might drop on his head from the sky," said the frivolous Herbert.

"Morris said the things happened so naturally," said' his father, "that you might if you so wished attribute it to coincidence."

"Well, don't break into the money before I come back," said Herbert as he rose from the table.

"I'm afraid it'll turn you into a mean, avaricious man, and we shall have to disown you."

His mother laughed, and following him to the door, watched him down the road; and returning to the breakfast table, was very happy at the expense of her husband's credulity. All of which did not prevent her from scurrying to the door at the postman's knock, nor prevent her from referring somewhat shortly to retired sergeant-majors of bibulous habits when she found that the post brought a tailor's bill.

"Herbert will have some more of his funny remarks, I expect, when he comes home," she said, as they sat at dinner.

"I dare say," said Mr. White, pouring himself out some beer; "but for all that, the thing moved in my hand; that I'll swear to."

"You thought it did," said the old lady soothingly.

"I say it did," replied the other. "There was no thought about it; I had just—What's the matter?"

His wife made no reply. She was watching the

mysterious movements of a man outside, who, peering in an undecided fashion at the house, appeared to be trying to make up his mind to enter. In mental connection with the two hundred pounds, she noticed that the stranger was well dressed, and wore a silk hat of glossy newness. Three times he paused at the gate, and then walked on again. The fourth time he stood with his hand upon it, and then with sudden resolution flung it open and walked up the path. Mrs. White at the same moment placed her hands behind her, and hurriedly unfastening the strings of her apron, put that useful article of apparel beneath the cushion of her chair.

She brought the stranger, who seemed ill at ease, into the room. He gazed at her furtively, and listened in a preoccupied fashion as the old lady apologized for the appearance of the room, and her husband's coat, a garment which he usually reserved for the garden. She then waited as patiently as her sex would permit, for him to broach his business, but he was at first strangely silent.

"I—was asked to call," he said at last, and stooped and picked a piece of cotton from his trousers. "I come from 'Maw and Meggins.'"

The old lady started. "Is anything the matter?" she asked, breathlessly. "Has anything happened to Herbert? What is it? What is it?"

Her husband interposed. "There, there, mother," he said, hastily. "Sit down, and don't jump to conclusions. You've not brought bad news, I'm sure, sir;" and he eyed the other wistfully.

"I'm sorry—" began the visitor.

"Is he hurt?" demanded the mother, wildly.

The visitor bowed in assent. "Badly hurt," he said, quietly, "but he is not in any pain."

"Oh, thank God!" said the old woman, clasping her hands. "Thank God for that! Thank—"

She broke off suddenly as the sinister meaning of the assurance dawned upon her and she saw the awful confirmation of her fears in the other's perverted face. She caught her breath, and turning to her slower-witted husband, laid her trembling old hand upon his.

There was a long silence.

"He was caught in the machinery," said the visitor at length in a low voice.

"Caught in the machinery," repeated Mr. White, in a dazed fashion, "yes."

He sat staring blankly out at the window, and taking his wife's hand between his own, pressed it as he had been wont to do in their old courting-days nearly forty years before.

"He was the only one left to us," he said, turning gently to the visitor. "It is hard."

The other coughed, and rising, walked slowly to the window. "The firm wished me to convey their sincere sympathy with you in your great loss," he said, without looking round. "I beg that you will understand I am only their servant and merely obeying orders."

There was no reply; the old woman's face was white, her eyes staring, and her breath inaudible; on the husband's face was a look such as his friend the sergeant might have carried into his first action.

"I was to say that Maw and Meggins disclaim all responsibility," continued the other. "They admit no liability at all, but in consideration of your son's services, they wish to present you with a certain sum as compensation."

Mr. White dropped his wife's hand, and rising to his feet, gazed with a look of horror at his visitor. His dry lips shaped the words, "How much?"

"Two hundred pounds," was the answer.

Unconscious of his wife's shriek, the old man smiled faintly, put out his hands like a sightless man, and dropped, a senseless heap, to the floor.

III

In the huge new cemetery, some two miles distant, the old people buried their dead, and came back to a house steeped in shadow and silence. It was all over so quickly that at first they could hardly realize it, and remained in a state of expectation as though of something else to happen—something else which was to lighten this load, too heavy for old hearts to bear.

But the days passed, and expectation gave place to resignation—the hopeless resignation of the old, sometimes miscalled, apathy. Sometimes they hardly exchanged a word, for now they had nothing to talk about, and their days were long to weariness.

It was about a week after that the old man, waking suddenly in the night, stretched out his hand and found himself alone. The room was in darkness, and the sound of subdued weeping came from the window. He raised himself in bed and listened.

"Come back," he said, tenderly. "You will be cold."

"It is colder for my son," said the old woman, and wept afresh.

The sound of her sobs died away on his ears. The bed was warm, and his eyes heavy with sleep. He dozed fitfully, and then slept until a sudden wild cry from his wife awoke him with a start.

"The paw!" she cried wildly. "The monkey's paw!"

He started up in alarm. "Where? Where is it? What's the matter?"

She came stumbling across the room toward him. "I want it," she said, quietly. "You've not destroyed it?"

"It's in the parlour, on the bracket," he replied, marvelling. "Why?"

She cried and laughed together, and bending over, kissed his cheek.

"I only just thought of it," she said, hysterically. "Why didn't I think of it before? Why didn't you think of it?"

"Think of what?" he questioned.

"The other two wishes," she replied, rapidly.

"We've only had one."

"Was not that enough?" he demanded, fiercely.

"No," she cried, triumphantly; "we'll have one more. Go down and get it quickly, and wish our boy alive again."

The man sat up in bed and flung the bedclothes from his quaking limbs. "Good God, you are mad!" he cried, aghast.

"Get it," she panted; "get it quickly, and wish—Oh, my boy, my boy!"

Her husband struck a match and lit the candle. "Get back to bed," he said, unsteadily. "You don't know what you are saying."

"We had the first wish granted," said the old woman, feverishly; "why not the second?"

"A coincidence," stammered the old man.

"Go and get it and wish," cried his wife, quivering with excitement.

The old man turned and regarded her, and his voice shook. "He has been dead ten days, and besides he—I would not tell you else, but—I could only recognize him by his clothing. If he was too terrible for you to see then, how now?"

"Bring him back," cried the old woman, and dragged him toward the door. "Do you think I fear the child I have nursed?"

He went down in the darkness, and felt his way to the parlour, and then to the mantelpiece. The talisman was in its place, and a horrible fear that the unspoken wish might bring his mutilated son before him ere he could escape from the room seized upon him, and he caught his breath as he found that he had lost the direction of the door. His brow cold with sweat, he felt his way round the table, and groped along the wall until he found himself in the small passage with the unwholesome thing in his hand.

Even his wife's face seemed changed as he entered the room. It was white and expectant, and to his fears seemed to have an unnatural look upon it. He was afraid of her.

"Wish!" she cried, in a strong voice.

"It is foolish and wicked," he faltered.

"Wish!" repeated his wife.

He raised his hand. "I wish my son alive again."

The talisman fell to the floor, and he regarded it fearfully. Then he sank trembling into a chair as the old woman, with burning eyes, walked to the window and raised the blind.

He sat until he was chilled with the cold, glancing occasionally at the figure of the old woman peering through the window. The candle-end, which had burned below the rim of the china candlestick, was throwing pulsating shadows on the ceiling and walls, until, with a flicker larger than the rest, it expired. The old man, with an unspeakable sense of relief at the failure of the talisman, crept back to his bed, and a minute or two afterward the old woman came silently and apathetically beside him.

Neither spoke, but lay silently listening to the ticking of the clock. A stair creaked, and a squeaky mouse scurried noisily through the wall. The darkness was oppressive, and after lying for some time screwing up his courage, he took the box of matches, and striking one, went downstairs for a candle.

At the foot of the stairs the match went out, and he paused to strike another; and at the same moment a knock, so quiet and stealthy as to be scarcely audible, sounded on the front door.

The matches fell from his hand and spilled in the passage. He stood motionless, his breath suspended until the knock was repeated. Then he turned and fled swiftly back to his room, and closed the door behind him. A third knock sounded through the house.

"What's that?" cried the old woman, starting up.

"A rat," said the old man in shaking tones—"a rat. It passed me on the stairs."

His wife sat up in bed listening. A loud knock resounded through the house.

"It's Herbert!" she screamed. "It's Herbert!"

She ran to the door, but her husband was

before her, and catching her by the arm, held her tightly.

"What are you going to do?" he whispered hoarsely.

"It's my boy; it's Herbert!" she cried, struggling mechanically. "I forgot it was two miles away. What are you holding me for? Let go. I must open the door.

"For God's sake don't let it in," cried the old man, trembling.

"You're afraid of your own son," she cried, struggling. "Let me go. I'm coming, Herbert; I'm coming."

There was another knock, and another. The old woman with a sudden wrench broke free and ran from the room. Her husband followed to the landing, and called after her appealingly as she hurried downstairs. He heard the chain rattle back and the bottom bolt drawn slowly and stiffly from the socket. Then the old woman's voice, strained and panting.

"The bolt," she cried, loudly. "Come down. I

can't reach it."

But her husband was on his hands and knees groping wildly on the floor in search of the paw. If he could only find it before the thing outside got in. A perfect fusillade of knocks reverberated through the house, and he heard the scraping of a chair as his wife put it down in the passage against the door. He heard the creaking of the bolt as it came slowly back, and at the same moment he found the monkey's paw, and frantically breathed his third and last wish.

The knocking ceased suddenly, although the echoes of it were still in the house. He heard the chair drawn back, and the door opened. A cold wind rushed up the staircase, and a long loud wail of disappointment and misery from his wife gave him courage to run down to her side, and then to the gate beyond. The street lamp flickering opposite shone on a quiet and deserted road.

THE GIFT OF THE MAGI

by O. Henry

One dollar and eighty-seven cents. That was all. And sixty cents of it was in pennies. Pennies saved one and two at a time by bulldozing the grocer and the vegetable man and the butcher until one's cheeks burned with the silent imputation of parsimony that such close dealing implied. Three times Della counted it. One dollar and eighty-seven cents. And the next day would be Christmas.

There was clearly nothing to do but flop down on the shabby little couch and howl. So Della did it. Which instigates the moral reflection that life is made up of sobs, sniffles, and smiles, with sniffles predominating.

While the mistress of the home is gradually subsiding from the first stage to the second, take a look at the home. A furnished flat at $8 per week. It did not exactly beggar description, but it certainly had that word on the lookout for the mendicancy squad.

In the vestibule below was a letter-box into which no letter would go, and an electric button from which no mortal finger could coax a ring. Also appertaining thereunto was a card bearing the name "Mr. James Dillingham Young."

The "Dillingham" had been flung to the breeze during a former period of prosperity when its possessor was being paid $30 per week. Now, when the income was shrunk to $20, though, they were thinking seriously of contracting to a modest and unassuming D. But whenever Mr. James Dillingham Young came home and reached his flat above he was called "Jim" and greatly hugged by Mrs. James Dillingham Young, already introduced to you as Della. Which is all very good.

Della finished her cry and attended to her cheeks with the powder rag. She stood by the window and looked out dully at a gray cat walking a gray fence in a gray backyard. Tomorrow would be Christmas

Day, and she had only $1.87 with which to buy Jim a present. She had been saving every penny she could for months, with this result. Twenty dollars a week doesn't go far. Expenses had been greater than she had calculated. They always are. Only $1.87 to buy a present for Jim. Her Jim. Many a happy hour she had spent planning for something nice for him. Something fine and rare and sterling—something just a little bit near to being worthy of the honor of being owned by Jim.

There was a pier-glass between the windows of the room. Perhaps you have seen a pierglass in an $8 flat. A very thin and very agile person may, by observing his reflection in a rapid sequence of longitudinal strips, obtain a fairly accurate conception of his looks. Della, being slender, had mastered the art.

Suddenly she whirled from the window and stood before the glass. her eyes were shining brilliantly, but her face had lost its color within twenty seconds. Rapidly she pulled down her hair and let it fall to its full length.

Now, there were two possessions of the James Dillingham Youngs in which they both took a mighty pride. One was Jim's gold watch that had been his father's and his grandfather's. The other was Della's hair. Had the queen of Sheba lived in the flat across the airshaft, Della would have let her hair hang out the window some day to dry just to depreciate Her Majesty's jewels and gifts. Had King Solomon been the janitor, with all his treasures piled up in the basement, Jim would have pulled out his watch every time he passed, just to see him pluck at his beard from envy.

So now Della's beautiful hair fell about her rippling and shining like a cascade of brown waters. It reached below her knee and made itself almost a garment for her. And then she did it up again nervously and quickly. Once she faltered for a minute and stood still while a tear or two splashed on the worn red carpet.

On went her old brown jacket; on went her old brown hat. With a whirl of skirts and with the brilliant sparkle still in her eyes, she fluttered out the door and down the stairs to the street.

Where she stopped the sign read: "Mne. Sofronie. Hair Goods of All Kinds." One flight up Della ran, and collected herself, panting. Madame, large, too white, chilly, hardly looked the "Sofronie."

"Will you buy my hair?" asked Della.

"I buy hair," said Madame. "Take yer hat off and let's have a sight at the looks of it."

Down rippled the brown cascade.

"Twenty dollars," said Madame, lifting the mass with a practised hand.

"Give it to me quick," said Della.

Oh, and the next two hours tripped by on rosy wings. Forget the hashed metaphor. She was ransacking the stores for Jim's present.

She found it at last. It surely had been made for Jim and no one else. There was no other like it in any of the stores, and she had turned all of them inside out. It was a platinum fob chain simple and chaste in design, properly proclaiming its value by substance alone and not by meretricious ornamentation—as all good things should do. It was even worthy of The Watch. As soon as she saw it she knew that it must be Jim's. It was like him. Quietness and value—the description applied to both. Twenty-one dollars they took from her for it, and she hurried home with the 87 cents. With that chain on his watch Jim might be properly anxious about the time in any company. Grand as the watch was, he sometimes looked at it on the sly on account of the old leather strap that he used in place of a chain.

When Della reached home her intoxication gave way a little to prudence and reason. She got out her curling irons and lighted the gas and went to work repairing the ravages made by generosity added to love. Which is always a tremendous task, dear friends—a mammoth task.

Within forty minutes her head was covered with tiny, close-lying curls that made her look wonderfully like a truant schoolboy. She looked at her reflection in the mirror long, carefully, and critically.

"If Jim doesn't kill me," she said to herself, "before he takes a second look at me, he'll say I look like a Coney Island chorus girl. But what could I do—oh! what could I do with a dollar and eighty-seven cents?"

At 7 o'clock the coffee was made and the frying-pan was on the back of the stove hot and ready to cook the chops.

Jim was never late. Della doubled the fob chain in her hand and sat on the corner of the table near the door that he always entered. Then she heard his step on the stair away down on the first flight, and she turned white for just a moment. She had a habit of saying a little silent prayer about the simplest everyday things, and now she whispered: "Please God, make him think I am still pretty."

The door opened and Jim stepped in and closed it. He looked thin and very serious. Poor fellow, he was only twenty-two—and to be burdened with a family! He needed a new overcoat and he was without gloves.

Jim stopped inside the door, as immovable as a setter at the scent of quail. His eyes were fixed upon Della, and there was an expression in them that she could not read, and it terrified her. It was not anger, nor surprise, nor disapproval, nor horror, nor any of the sentiments that she had been prepared for. He simply stared at her fixedly with that peculiar expression on his face.

Della wriggled off the table and went for him.

"Jim, darling," she cried, "don't look at me that way. I had my hair cut off and sold because I couldn't have lived through Christmas without giving you a present. It'll grow out again—you won't mind, will you? I just had to do it. My hair grows awfully fast. Say `Merry Christmas!' Jim, and let's be happy. You don't know what a nice—what a beautiful, nice gift I've got for you."

"You've cut off your hair?" asked Jim, laboriously, as if he had not arrived at that patent fact yet even after the hardest mental labor.

"Cut it off and sold it," said Della. "Don't you

like me just as well, anyhow? I'm me without my hair, ain't I?"

Jim looked about the room curiously.

"You say your hair is gone?" he said, with an air almost of idiocy.

"You needn't look for it," said Della. "It's sold, I tell you—sold and gone, too. It's Christmas Eve, boy. Be good to me, for it went for you. Maybe the hairs of my head were numbered," she went on with sudden serious sweetness, "but nobody could ever count my love for you. Shall I put the chops on, Jim?"

Out of his trance Jim seemed quickly to wake. He enfolded his Della. For ten seconds let us regard with discreet scrutiny some inconsequential object in the other direction. Eight dollars a week or a million a year—what is the difference? A mathematician or a wit would give you the wrong answer. The magi brought valuable gifts, but that was not among them. This dark assertion will be illuminated later on.

Jim drew a package from his overcoat pocket and threw it upon the table.

"Don't make any mistake, Dell," he said, "about me. I don't think there's anything in the way of a haircut or a shave or a shampoo that could make me like my girl any less. But if you'll unwrap that package you may see why you had me going a while at first."

White fingers and nimble tore at the string and paper. And then an ecstatic scream of joy; and then, alas! a quick feminine change to hysterical tears and wails, necessitating the immediate employment of all the comforting powers of the lord of the flat.

For there lay The Combs—the set of combs, side and back, that Della had worshipped long in a Broadway window. Beautiful combs, pure tortoise shell, with jewelled rims—just the shade to wear in the beautiful vanished hair. They were expensive combs, she knew, and her heart had simply craved and yearned over them without the least hope of possession. And now, they were hers, but the tresses that should have adorned the coveted adornments were gone.

But she hugged them to her bosom, and at length she was able to look up with dim eyes and a smile and say: "My hair grows so fast, Jim!"

And then Della leaped up like a little singed cat and cried, "Oh, oh!"

Jim had not yet seen his beautiful present. She held it out to him eagerly upon her open palm. The dull precious metal seemed to flash with a reflection of her bright and ardent spirit.

"Isn't it a dandy, Jim? I hunted all over town to find it. You'll have to look at the time a hundred times a day now. Give me your watch. I want to see how it looks on it."

Instead of obeying, Jim tumbled down on the couch and put his hands under the back of his head and smiled.

"Dell," said he, "let's put our Christmas presents away and keep 'em a while. They're too nice to use just at present. I sold the watch to get the money to buy your combs. And now suppose you put the chops on."

The magi, as you know, were wise men—wonderfully wise men—who brought gifts to the Babe in the manger. They invented the art of giving Christmas presents. Being wise, their gifts were no doubt wise ones, possibly bearing the privilege of exchange in case of duplication. And here I have lamely related to you the uneventful chronicle of two foolish children in a flat who most unwisely sacrificed for each other the greatest treasures of their house. But in a last word to the wise of these days let it be said that of all who give gifts these two were the wisest. Of all who give and receive gifts, such as they are wisest. Everywhere they are wisest. They are the magi.

THE RANSOM OF RED CHIEF

by O. Henry

It looked like a good thing: but wait till I tell you. We were down South, in Alabama—Bill Driscoll and myself—when this kidnapping idea struck us. It was, as Bill afterward expressed it, "during a moment of temporary mental apparition"; but we didn't find that out till later.

There was a town down there, as flat as a flannel-cake, and called Summit, of course. It contained inhabitants of as undeleterious and self-satisfied a class of peasantry as ever clustered around a Maypole.

Bill and me had a joint capital of about six hundred dollars, and we needed just two thousand dollars more to pull off a fraudulent town-lot scheme in Western Illinois with. We talked it over on the front steps of the hotel. Philoprogenitiveness, says we, is strong in semi-rural communities; therefore, and for other reasons, a kidnaping project ought to do better there than in the radius of newspapers that send reporters out in plain clothes to stir up talk about such things. We knew that Summit couldn't get after us with anything stronger than constables and, maybe, some lackadaisical bloodhounds and a diatribe or two in the *Weekly Farmers' Budget.* So, it looked good.

We selected for our victim the only child of a prominent citizen named Ebenezer Dorset. The father was respectable and tight, a mortgage fancier and a stern, upright collection-plate passer and forecloser. The kid was a boy of ten, with bas-relief freckles, and hair the color of the cover of the magazine you buy at the news-stand when you want to catch a train. Bill and me figured that Ebenezer would melt down for a ransom of two thousand dollars to a cent. But wait till I tell you.

About two miles from Summit was a little mountain, covered with a dense cedar brake. On the rear elevation of this mountain was a cave. There we stored provisions.

One evening after sundown, we drove in a buggy past old Dorset's house. The kid was in the street, throwing rocks at a kitten on the opposite fence.

"Hey, little boy!" says Bill, "would you like to have a bag of candy and a nice ride?"

The boy catches Bill neatly in the eye with a piece of brick.

"That will cost the old man an extra five hundred dollars," says Bill, climbing over the wheel.

That boy put up a fight like a welter-weight cinnamon bear; but, at last, we got him down in the bottom of the buggy and drove away. We took him up to the cave, and I hitched the horse in the cedar brake. After dark I drove the buggy to the little village, three miles away, where we had hired it, and walked back to the mountain.

Bill was pasting court-plaster over the scratches and bruises on his features. There was a fire burning behind the big rock at the entrance of the cave, and the boy was watching a pot of boiling coffee, with two buzzard tail-feathers stuck in his red hair. He points a stick at me when I come up, and says:

"Ha! cursed paleface, do you dare to enter the camp of Red Chief, the terror of the plains?"

"He's all right now," says Bill, rolling up his trousers and examining some bruises on his shins. "We're playing Indian. We're making Buffalo Bill's show look like magic-lantern views of Palestine in the town hall. I'm Old Hank, the Trapper, Red Chief's captive, and I'm to be scalped at daybreak. By Geronimo! that kid can kick hard."

Yes, sir, that boy seemed to be having the time of his life. The fun of camping out in a cave had made him forget that he was a captive himself. He immediately christened me Snake-eye, the Spy, and announced that, when his braves returned from the warpath, I was to be broiled at the stake at the rising of the sun.

Then we had supper; and he filled his mouth full of bacon and bread and gravy, and began to talk.

He made a during-dinner speech something like this:

"I like this fine. I never camped out before; but I had a pet 'possum once, and I was nine last birthday. I hate to go to school. Rats ate up sixteen of Jimmy Talbot's aunt's speckled hen's eggs. Are there any real Indians in these woods? I want some more gravy. Does the trees moving make the wind blow? We had five puppies. What makes your nose so red, Hank? My father has lots of money. Are the stars hot? I whipped Ed Walker twice, Saturday. I don't like girls. You dassent catch toads unless with a string. Do oxen make any noise? Why are oranges round? Have you got beds to sleep on in this cave? Amos Murray has got six toes. A parrot can talk, but a monkey or a fish can't. How many does it take to make twelve?"

Every few minutes he would remember that he was a pesky redskin, and pick up his stick rifle and tiptoe to the mouth of the cave to rubber for the scouts of the hated paleface. Now and then he would let out a war-whoop that made Old Hank the Trapper shiver. That boy had Bill terrorized from the start.

"Red Chief," says I to the kid, "would you like to go home?"

"Aw, what for?" says he. "I don't have any fun at home. I hate to go to school. I like to camp out. You won't take me back home again, Snake-eye, will you?"

"Not right away," says I. "We'll stay here in the cave a while."

"All right!" says he. "That'll be fine. I never had such fun in all my life."

We went to bed about eleven o'clock. We spread down some wide blankets and quilts and put Red Chief between us. We weren't afraid he'd run away. He kept us awake for three hours, jumping up and reaching for his rifle and screeching: "Hist! pard," in mine and Bill's ears, as the fancied crackle of a twig or the rustle of a leaf revealed to his young imagination the stealthy approach of the outlaw band. At last, I fell into a troubled sleep, and dreamed that I had been kidnapped and chained to a tree by a ferocious pirate with red hair.

Just at daybreak, I was awakened by a series of awful screams from Bill. They weren't yells, or howls, or shouts, or whoops, or yawps, such as you'd expect from a manly set of vocal organs—they were simply indecent, terrifying, humiliating screams, such as women emit when they see ghosts or caterpillars. It's an awful thing to hear a strong, desperate, fat man scream incontinently in a cave at daybreak.

I jumped up to see what the matter was. Red Chief was sitting on Bill's chest, with one hand twined in Bill's hair. In the other he had the sharp case-knife we used for slicing bacon; and he was industriously and realistically trying to take Bill's scalp, according to the sentence that had been pronounced upon him the evening before.

I got the knife away from the kid and made him lie down again. But, from that moment, Bill's spirit was broken. He laid down on his side of the bed, but he never closed an eye again in sleep as long as that boy was with us. I dozed off for a while, but along toward sun-up I remembered that Red Chief had said I was to be burned at the stake at the rising of the sun. I wasn't nervous or afraid; but I sat up and lit my pipe and leaned against a rock.

"What you getting up so soon for, Sam?" asked Bill.

"Me?" says I. "Oh, I got a kind of a pain in my shoulder. I thought sitting up would rest it."

"You're a liar!" says Bill. "You're afraid. You was to be burned at sunrise, and you was afraid he'd do it. And he would, too, if he could find a match. Ain't it awful, Sam? Do you think anybody will pay out

money to get a little imp like that back home?"

"Sure," said I. "A rowdy kid like that is just the kind that parents dote on. Now, you and the Chief get up and cook breakfast, while I go up on the top of this mountain and reconnoiter."

I went up on the peak of the little mountain and ran my eye over the contiguous vicinity. Over toward Summit I expected to see the sturdy yeomanry of the village armed with scythes and pitchforks beating the countryside for the dastardly kidnapers. But what I saw was a peaceful landscape dotted with one man ploughing with a dun mule. Nobody was dragging the creek; no couriers dashed hither and yon, bringing tidings of no news to the distracted parents. There was a sylvan attitude of somnolent sleepiness pervading that section of the external outward surface of Alabama that lay exposed to my view. "Perhaps," says I to myself, "it has not yet been discovered that the wolves have borne away the tender lambkin from the fold. Heaven help the wolves!" says I, and I went down the mountain to breakfast.

When I got to the cave I found Bill backed up against the side of it, breathing hard, and the boy threatening to smash him with a rock half as big as a cocoanut.

"He put a red-hot boiled potato down my back," explained Bill, "and then mashed it with his foot; and I boxed his ears. Have you got a gun about you, Sam?"

I took the rock away from the boy and kind of

patched up the argument. "I'll fix you," says the kid to Bill. "No man ever yet struck the Red Chief but what he got paid for it. You better beware!"

After breakfast the kid takes a piece of leather with strings wrapped around it out of his pocket and goes outside the cave unwinding it.

"What's he up to now?" says Bill anxiously. "You don't think he'll run away, do you, Sam?"

"No fear of it," says I. "He don't seem to be much of a home body. But we've got to fix up some plan about the ransom. There don't seem to be much excitement around Summit on account of his disappearance; but maybe they haven't realized yet that he's gone. His folks may think he's spending the night with Aunt Jane or one of the neighbors. Anyhow, he'll

be missed to-day. To-night we must get a message to his father demanding the two thousand dollars for his return."

Just then we heard a kind of war-whoop, such as David might have emitted when he knocked out the champion Goliath. It was a sling that Red Chief had pulled out of his pocket, and he was whirling it around his head.

I dodged, and heard a heavy thud and a kind of a sigh from Bill, like a horse gives out when you take his saddle off. A niggerhead rock the size of an egg had caught Bill just behind his left ear. He loosened himself all over and fell in the fire across the frying pan of hot water for washing the dishes. I dragged him out and poured cold water on his head for half an hour.

By and by, Bill sits up and feels behind his ear and says: "Sam, do you know who my favorite Biblical character is?"

"Take it easy," says I. "You'll come to your senses presently."

"King Herod," says he. "You won't go away and leave me here alone, will you, Sam?"

I went out and caught that boy and shook him until his freckles rattled.

"If you don't behave," says I, "I'll take you

straight home. Now, are you going to be good, or not?"

"I was only funning," says he sullenly. "I didn't mean to hurt Old Hank. But what did he hit me for? I'll behave, Snake-eye, if you won't send me home, and if you'll let me play the Black Scout to-day."

"I don't know the game," says I. "That's for you and Mr. Bill to decide. He's your playmate for the day. I'm going away for a while, on business. Now, you come in and make friends with him and say you are sorry for hurting him, or home you go, at once."

I made him and Bill shake hands, and then I took Bill aside and told him I was going to Poplar Cove, a little village three miles from the cave, and find out what I could about how the kidnapping had been regarded in Summit. Also, I thought it best to send a peremptory letter to old man Dorset that day, demanding the ransom and dictating how it should be paid.

"You know, Sam," says Bill, "I've stood by you without batting an eye in earthquakes, fire, and flood—in poker games, dynamite outrages, police raids, train robberies, and cyclones. I never lost my nerve yet till we kidnapped that two-legged skyrocket of a kid. He's got me going. You won't leave me long with him, will you, Sam?"

"I'll be back some time this afternoon," says I. "You must keep the boy amused and quiet till I return. And now we'll write the letter to old Dorset."

Bill and I got paper and pencil and worked on the letter while Red Chief, with a blanket wrapped around him, strutted up and down, guarding the mouth of the cave. Bill begged me tearfully to make the ransom fifteen hundred dollars instead of two thousand. "I ain't attempting," says he, "to decry the celebrated moral aspect of parental affection, but we're dealing with humans, and it ain't human for anybody to give up two thousand dollars for that forty-pound chunk of freckled wildcat. I'm willing to take a chance at fifteen hundred dollars. You can charge the difference up to me."

So, to relieve Bill, I acceded, and we

collaborated a letter that ran this way:

"Ebenezer Dorset, Esq.:

We have your boy concealed in a place far from Summit. It is useless for you or the most skillful detectives to attempt to find him. Absolutely, the only terms on which you can have him restored to you are these: We demand fifteen hundred dollars in large bills for his return; the money to be left at midnight to-night at the same spot and in the same box as your reply—as hereinafter described. If you agree to these terms, send your answer in writing by a solitary messenger to-night at half-past eight o'clock. After crossing Owl Creek, on the road to Poplar Cove, there are three large trees about a hundred yards apart, close to the fence of the wheat field on the right-hand side. At the bottom of the fence-post, opposite the third tree, will be found a small paste-board box.

The messenger will place the answer in this box and return immediately to Summit.

If you attempt any treachery or fail to comply

with our demand as stated, you will never see your boy again.

If you pay the money as demanded, he will be returned to you safe and well within three hours.

These terms are final, and if you do not accede to them no further communication will be attempted.

TWO DESPERATE MEN."

I addressed this letter to Dorset, and put it in my pocket. As I was about to start, the kid comes up to me and says:

"Aw, Snake-eye, you said I could play the Black Scout while you was gone."

"Play it, of course," says I. "Mr. Bill will play with you. What kind of a game is it?"

"I'm the Black Scout," says Red Chief, "and I have to ride to the stockade to warn the settlers that the Indians are coming. I'm tired of playing Indian myself. I want to be the Black Scout."

"All right," says I. "It sounds harmless to me. I guess Mr. Bill will help you foil the pesky savages."

"What am I to do?" asks Bill, looking at the kid suspiciously.

"You are the hoss," says Black Scout. "Get down on your hands and knees. How can I ride to the stockade without a hoss?"

"You'd better keep him interested," said I, "till we get the scheme going. Loosen up."

Bill gets down on his all fours, and a look comes in his eye like a rabbit's when you catch it in a trap.

"How far is it to the stockade, kid?" he asks, in a husky manner of voice.

"Ninety miles," says the Black Scout. "And you have to hump yourself to get there on time. Whoa, now!"

The Black Scout jumps on Bill's back and digs his heels in his side.

"For Heaven's sake," says Bill, "hurry back, Sam, as soon as you can. I wish we hadn't made the ransom more than a thousand. Say, you quit kicking me or I'll get up and warm you good."

I walked over to Poplar Cove and sat around the post-office and store, talking with the chawbacons that came in to trade. One whiskerando says that he hears Summit is all upset on account of Elder Ebenezer Dorset's boy having been lost or stolen. That was all I wanted to know. I bought some smoking tobacco, referred casually to the price of black-eyed peas, posted my letter surreptitiously, and came away. The postmaster said the mail-carrier would come by in an hour to take the mail on to Summit.

When I got back to the cave Bill and the boy were not to be found. I explored the vicinity of the cave, and risked a yodel or two, but there was no response.

So I lighted my pipe and sat down on a mossy bank to await developments.

In about half an hour I heard the bushes rustle, and Bill wabbled out into the little glade in front of the cave. Behind him was the kid, stepping softly like a scout, with a broad grin on his face. Bill stopped, took off his hat, and wiped his face with a red handkerchief. The kid stopped about eight feet behind him.

"Sam," says Bill, "I suppose you'll think I'm a renegade, but I couldn't help it. I'm a grown person with masculine proclivities and habits of self-defense, but there is a time when all systems of egotism and predominance fail. The boy is gone. I have sent him home. All is off. There was martyrs in old times," goes on Bill, "that suffered death rather than give up the particular graft they enjoyed. None of 'em ever was subjugated to such supernatural tortures as I have been. I tried to be faithful to our articles of depredation; but there came a limit."

"What's the trouble, Bill?" I asks him.

"I was rode," says Bill, "the ninety miles to the stockade, not barring an inch. Then, when the settlers was rescued, I was given oats. Sand ain't a palatable substitute. And then, for an hour I had to try to explain to him why there was nothin' in holes, how a road can run both ways, and what makes the grass green. I tell you, Sam, a human can only stand so much. I takes him by the neck of his clothes and drags him down the mountain. On the way he kicks my legs black-and-blue from the knees down; and I've got to have two or three bites on my thumb and hand cauterized.

"But he's gone"—continues Bill—"gone home. I showed him the road to Summit and kicked him about eight feet nearer there at one kick. I'm sorry we lose the ransom; but it was either that or Bill Driscoll to the madhouse."

Bill is puffing and blowing, but there is a look of ineffable peace and growing content on his rose-pink features.

"Bill," says I, "there isn't any heart disease in your family, is there?"

"No," says Bill, "nothing chronic except malaria and accidents. Why?"

"Then you might turn around," says I, "and have a look behind you."

Bill turns and sees the boy, and loses his complexion and sits down plump on the ground and begins to pluck aimlessly at grass and little sticks. For an hour I was afraid for his mind. And then I told him that my scheme was to put the whole job through immediately and that we would get the ransom and be off with it by midnight if old Dorset fell in with our proposition. So Bill braced up enough to give the kid a weak sort of a smile and a promise to play the Russian in a Japanese war with him as soon as he felt a little better.

I had a scheme for collecting that ransom without danger of being caught by counterplots that ought to commend itself to professional kidnapers. The tree under which the answer was to be left—and the money later on—was close to the road fence with big, bare fields on all sides. If a gang of constables should be watching for any one to come for the note, they could see him a long way off crossing the fields or in the road. But no, siree! At half-past eight I was up in that tree as well hidden as a tree toad, waiting for the messenger to arrive.

Exactly on time, a half-grown boy rides up the

road on a bicycle, locates the pasteboard box at the foot of the fence-post, slips a folded piece of paper into it, and pedals away again back toward Summit.

I waited an hour and then concluded the thing was square. I slid down the tree, got the note, slipped along the fence till I struck the woods, and was back at the cave in another half an hour. I opened the note, got near the lantern, and read it to Bill. It was written with a pen in a crabbed hand, and the sum and substance of it was this:

"Two Desperate Men.

Gentlemen: I received your letter to-day by post, in regard to the ransom you ask for the return of my son. I think you are a little high in your demands, and I hereby make you a counter-proposition, which I am inclined to believe you will accept. You bring Johnny home and pay me two hundred and fifty dollars in cash, and I agree to take him off your hands. You had better come at night, for the neighbors believe he is lost, and I couldn't be responsible for what they would do to anybody they saw bringing him back.

Very respectfully,

EBENEZER DORSET."

"Great pirates of Penzance!" says I; "of all the impudent—"

But I glanced at Bill, and hesitated. He had the most appealing look in his eyes I ever saw on the face of a dumb or a talking brute.

"Sam," says he, "what's two hundred and fifty dollars, after all? We've got the money. One more night of this kid will send me to a bed in Bedlam. Besides being a thorough gentleman, I think Mr. Dorset is a spendthrift for making us such a liberal offer. You ain't going to let the chance go, are you?"

"Tell you the truth, Bill," says I, "this little he ewe lamb has somewhat got on my nerves too. We'll take him home, pay the ransom, and make our getaway."

We took him home that night. We got him to

go by telling him that his father had bought a silver-mounted rifle and a pair of moccasins for him, and we were going to hunt bears the next day.

It was just twelve o'clock when we knocked at Ebenezer's front door. Just at the moment when I should have been abstracting the fifteen hundred dollars from the box under the tree, according to the original proposition, Bill was counting out two hundred and fifty dollars into Dorset's hand.

When the kid found out we were going to leave him at home he started up a howl like a calliope and fastened himself as tight as a leech to Bill's leg. His father peeled him away gradually, like a porous plaster.

"How long can you hold him!" asks Bill.

"I'm not as strong as I used to be," says old Dorset, "but I think I can promise you ten minutes."

"Enough," says Bill. "In ten minutes I shall cross the Central, Southern, and Middle Western States, and be legging it trippingly for the Canadian border."

And, as dark as it was, and as fat as Bill was, and as good a runner as I am, he was a good mile and a half out of Summit before I could catch up with him.

www.ingramcontent.com/pod-product-compliance
Lightning Source LLC
Chambersburg PA
CBHW032119020726
47494CB00007BA/2140
* 9 7 8 1 4 7 3 3 1 1 2 6 8 *